Streetwise

They clung to each other on the roof, swaying
drunkenly with the frost gleaming hard on the
skylights. Above them, a crescent moon was
etched against the swollen clouds that raced
across the chill darkness of the night sky. . . .

'What's in there then?'
'Fags and booze, man. Tons of fags and
booze.'

ANTHONY MASTERS

Streetwise

Methuen

To Miriam

First published in 1987
by Methuen Children's Books Ltd
This Methuen Teens paperback first published 1988
by Methuen Children's Books
A Division of OPG Services Ltd
Michelin House, 81 Fulham Road, London SW3 6RB
Copyright © 1987 Anthony Masters
Printed in Great Britain

ISBN 0–416–10152–6

Contents

Part One
Dead Men's Shoes

They clung to each other on the roof, swaying drunkenly with the frost gleaming hard on the skylights. Above them, a crescent moon was etched against the swollen clouds that raced across the chill darkness of the night sky. Below them, an occasional vehicle nosed up the High Road, emitting a tiny, distant sound. A dog barked some distance away and a sharp wind rattled dustbins on the balconies of the flats just behind them. Alcohol protected both of them from freezing reality as they hushed one another into silence.

'What's in there then?'

'Fags and booze, man. Tons of fags and booze.'

'I'm goin' down.' Lloyd reeled slightly, only to be steadied by his companion.

'Listen – we're both goin' down,' snapped Wes.

He pulled out his knife and began to chip away at the sides of the glass. But nothing gave and the cold suddenly penetrated his fingers. He howled in protest.

'What's up?'

'It's cold.'

'Let's have a go.' But the putty remained frozen.

'We'll have to break the glass.' Lloyd's voice was thick, punctured by gasping bursts of laughter. Soon they were both at it. 'Give me that brick.' Wes hit the glass savagely, but nothing happened.

'Harder.'

Still nothing happened.

'Thump the bastard.'

The glass broke with a sudden clamour.

'That's loud, man.' Wes stumbled over the words.

They both looked down into the dark void wondering who would be first to make the perilous descent, but then their confidence returned and the alcohol buoyed them up again.

Sam was looking forward to the night fishing under Ramsgate Pier, with the girders and galleries covered with dozens of winking tilly lamps. It was like the palace of a medieval warrior prince that he had once seen in a fantasy film. The water lapped around the girders, and somewhere out at sea they would hear the mournful sound of the Goodwin beacon. As he gradually fell asleep, Sam suddenly caught a fleeting image of the glistening wet sands, exposed at low tide, with the knights drawn up in black ranks facing each other, waiting for the fight.

'Suspects now on roof of Wineland Supermarket, Elkin Road. Possibly kids. Over.'

The area car waited in the shadows, lights doused. The radio crackled quietly.

'Tango Three. Do you require assistance? Over.'

'Affirmative. We require assistance. Location left from Percy Street into Blenheim Mews. No horns.'

'On your way, Colin.'

Colin stole out of the police car gently, despite his height, crouched low and ran across the road to the black shape of the building opposite. For a moment he paused in the shadows and then began slowly to work his way to the rear of the delapidated building that housed the Wineland Supermarket.

'That's got it.'

Wes had noisily broken the rest of the glass and was chipping away at the jagged pieces round the edge of the skylight.

'Wish we'd got a torch.' Lloyd paused.

'Who needs a torch?' asked Wes.

Lloyd peered down, swaying slightly and steadying himself by placing both hands on the felt roofing.

'There's a false ceiling down there,' Lloyd whispered. 'I'll crawl over the top and find a way down.'

'Will it take your weight?' Wes asked.

'Sure.' Lloyd gave another half-smothered shriek. 'I'm going feet first. It's the only way.' He hesitated as if still half-decided and then plunged forward.

'Hang on . . .'

'See you.'

Lloyd dived and rolled over. The sense of foreboding hit him like a rock and he suddenly sobered up. But it was too late. A few seconds later a tearing, rending sound funnelled up through the skylight and it was accompanied by a half-human cry of fear and pain. There was a short silence. Then up through the skylight came the sound of hell, animal-like in the dark below. It seemed to last for ages until it changed to a keening that was even more painful to hear.

'Lloyd!' Wes bellowed again and again and again.

Sam was having another nightmare. Gone were all the semi-waking dreams of Ramsgate and fishing and princes and sands and knights. Instead he saw Albino Man. His livid white face glowed deathly pale in the frosty darkness and his gingery Afro locks looked like rusty fire under the pallid moon. Sam was on one side of the pond on Clapham Common and Albino Man was on the other, racing towards him through the jagged icy night, cutting a red fire path on the whitened grass that shone in the moonlight. Then like in all dreams, Sam slipped on the wet grass and came down hard on spiky frost.

Colin broke open the side door of Wineland and listened to the agonising noise inside. Picking his way through the racks with a flashlight, he cautiously walked towards the sound. Blood was welling from something lying and moving slightly on the floor just beside a big display stand of Bull's Blood Hungarian Wine. For a moment Colin wondered if it was wine and not blood that was dribbling over the concrete floor. He flashed his torch and then moved away with an abrupt little cry. His heart began to thump unmercifully. He wanted to be sick.

    'Lloyd,' he whispered.

Sam lay helplessly on the frosty grass as Albino Man crept closer and closer towards him. Soon he was standing over him, his pinky eyes angry, his breath like wispy steam.

    'I want your heart,' he growled, and sent long spiky fingers down towards Sam's chest. 'I want to eat your heart out, man.'

The dark face of the boy stared up, his lips clenched in agony. Most of the blood seemed to be coming from somewhere round the back of his head and Colin dared not touch him.

    'So it's you then.' Lloyd stuttered faintly.
    'I'm here to help you, son.'
    'I don't want no help from you.'

Colin took out his pocket radio and sent out a call for assistance but then he saw something. 'Oi!'

Someone was running towards a staircase. Instantly, Colin knew the boy was going back on the roof. The sudden lights of the police car outside told him every possible escape route was cut off. As the others rushed towards him, Colin stared down at Lloyd. 'Arnie,' he shouted. 'There's a kid in here hurt real bad. I've radioed for an ambulance. Stay with him till they come. The other kid's up on the roof. I'm going after him.'

Arnie nodded as other policemen, together with a couple of tracker dogs, crowded into the supermarket. They formed a semi-circle round Lloyd, looking down at him with a strange mixture of anger and pity.

As Albino Man's fingers made searing contact with Sam's stomach, he woke up yelling. A few seconds later Mum cane in to find him still yelling. She frowned. This was happening too much. Sam opened his screwed-up eyes to see her reassuring nightdress. Her cigarette glowed faintly in the dark, and for an awful moment Sam was reminded of Albino Man's eyes.

'Dreaming again?'

'Yeah.'

'Albino Man?'

Sam nodded. In another room he could hear his brother Tim stirring and calling out.

'Wait,' Mum bellowed. 'I can't be in two places at once.' She looked down at Sam again with a kind of rough compassion. Mary Swallow was not one to show her feelings. She was shy, although neither of her children recognised that.

There was sweat on Sam's face and she wiped at it with the corner of a blanket. He's fourteen. He's going to be a man soon, she thought in sudden despair. She felt that the boys were growing away from her, even ten-year-old Tim. Growing away from her and growing nearer Colin. The man of action. Always taking them fishing and encouraging them to play in the football team that he ran as part of the Police Force's goodwill drive. What had she got to offer the boys? An office cleaner working for the extras Colin's policeman's pay couldn't afford. A reserved woman who had always wanted a daughter, too. It wasn't fair. Meanwhile she couldn't even comfort Sam. Couldn't even stop him dreaming this dream. Of course she had discussed it with Colin, but he said it wasn't important. He didn't think dreams were.

'Stay where you are, son.'

Wes moved away from the skylight and stood facing Colin in a half-crouching position.

'Wesley.' Colin spoke the name quietly. He had known all along who the other boy must be. Wes and Lloyd were inseparable. They were always in trouble and Wes was on a suspended sentence, despite all the efforts Colin, their community policeman, had made.

The boy moved a few steps backwards.

'Wesley.' Colin repeated his name and the boy edged backwards again.

'You're not getting me, honky.' The voice was a snarl.

'Lloyd's down there. He's hurt bad.'

'You think I don't know that.'

'Then come down with me.'

Colin wanted to keep him talking. The boy had to stay calm.

But it was Wesley who seemed to have all the chat.

'Listen, copper. Listen to the way you are. They all reckon you're the good guy. Football for the kids.
6

Outings for the little villains. Good straight talks, like, for the big villains. You're a right credit to the Old Bill, aren't you, honky? Least that's how it looks. If only they really knew what you'd been up to, eh? What about my auntie then? You kept that a good secret, didn't you, honky?'

'You stay where you are.' A blind anger had seized Colin and he lunged out at him, but Wesley ducked and weaved around the ventilation cowl.

'What you gonna do, honky? Knock me off the roof?'

Colin tried for calm but only just succeeded.

'Don't move,' he whispered. 'Please don't move.'

'Bastard – you been goin' with my auntie, and she never told me. You should be real ashamed of that. You a white pig and my auntie a widow. A poor helpless widow.'

Colin lunged forward again and Wesley laughed and dodged.

Wesley was now dangerously near the edge of the roof and Colin shouted:

'Just don't move again. Do you hear me?'

'I hear you, honky.'

Still Wesley moved back and Colin knew that his chances were running out. With a sudden movement, Colin threw himself forward and tried to grab him round the waist. But he was a fraction too late and Wesley fell over the top.

'Where's Dad?'

'Out on the beat. He won't be back till morning.' As she spoke Mary knew how triumphant she must sound. Why couldn't she just go to Sam and cuddle and kiss him. After all, his father did, big as Sam was. In fact he and the boys had never stopped cuddling and kissing. Of course Colin didn't do it in public, but directly he got the boys home he was at it again, whereas she seemed to touch them less and less. Her goodnight kisses hardly brushed against their cheeks and they barely seemed to respond at all. If only she wasn't so shy, if only she had Colin's confidence, if only she believed in herself, if only she could accept that other people could like her. That's what they had all said. And, in particular, that was what Colin had said, night after night. And he hadn't said it so nicely either. So in many ways she hadn't minded when he found his fancy woman, his little bit on the side. She had not known who she was for years. But now that she did know, Mary was terribly shocked. How could he have been so stupid? she wondered. How could a copper have chosen a black woman? It was a miracle there hadn't been trouble before. But what hurt her was the deception, all the hard work they must both have put into keeping it so secret. The meetings out of Stockwell, the little holidays, their stolen time. In the early days his fancy bits had made her feel safe, for they had made him good-tempered and she knew that he would never leave her. Not while the boys were growing up anyway. And after that . . . well, she couldn't think that far ahead. As long as Colin was around and doing everything for her she didn't have to snap out of being a nobody.

Sam looked round his square box-like little room. It was safely the same. No Albino Man in the corner. Instead there were the usual piles of comics and posters, football and swimming certificates, a pile of discarded Lego, the old shabby Teddy (called Ted now but secretly whispered to as Teddy), his football scarf, his Doc Marten boots, his portable TV; it was all the same. But not the same. Because Dad wasn't sitting on the edge of the bed and Mum was.

Tim shouted out again and Mum shouted back. Sam couldn't make out what it was but it sounded threatening and it certainly shut Tim up. She bent over Sam and he could smell her usual scent. It smelt like cherries mixed with pork pie. She always smelt like that. Always. Her big lips hesitantly brushed his cheek as he turned his head away.

'That Albino Man. He can't help the way he looks. There's no cause to be scared, Sam. You should pity him.' She knew that she wasn't using the right words, but suddenly Mary felt desperately tired. 'Get some sleep, I'll be next door.'

'Mum?'

'Yes?' Her voice was weary and subdued.

'It's football tomorrow.'

'Mmm.'

'Dad says we're going to thrash Thornton Heath.'

She nodded rather dismally.

'Then Dad's taking us fishing.'

'Tim's got a bit of a cold . . .'

'Let him come.'

She smiled gravely. 'I probably will.'

'You goin' to Bingo?'

'Maybe.'

'We're goin' fishing off the rocks as well as the pier.'

'Mmm. Goodnight then.'

'Night, Mum.' Sam lay back in his cramped bed, wondering if she would remember to tuck in his toes that were sticking out. But she didn't. He closed his eyes and the features of Albino Man swam into his mind. But then he pulled a trick that he had pulled before. In his waking dream, Sam leapt up at Albino Man and pulled at his scraggy cheek. It peeled off to reveal Dad's reassuring smile underneath.

The match had been good and Sam had scored a goal. He usually played right attack in the team but had had to win his place. 'I'm not playing you just because you're one of mine,' Dad had told him ages ago. And he was as good as his word, for when Sam had gone through a bad patch and hadn't got stuck in on the tackling, Dad had dropped him. Sam then had to work very hard at the training to get picked again. Dad was too busy being a copper to run the training nights down at the school on a Friday, so Wesley ran them for him. He was a brilliant player and was being considered for West Ham. Wesley was a good trainer, kind but tough when necessary, and he made it fun as well. He was tall and kicked the ball with a certain grace.

Wesley sometimes stood on the touchline on a Sunday morning, but this time he wasn't there. Dad seemed quiet and he didn't shout with his usual roar. Even when he was briefing them at half-time he didn't seem quite with it somehow. Tim had noticed too and he mentioned it to Sam, but Sam told him to shut up anyway as he often did.

But now they were down at Ramsgate. It was a wintry afternoon and as they sat under the girders of the pier the sea was red and gold underneath the hard little blob of a red sun. It was very calm and the water looked as if it were made of a kind of silky steel instead of sea. The sky was a kind of cold hard blue and there were hardly any clouds. It was a scene that Sam was going to remember all his life and for some reason he kept staring out to sea as if he was waiting for something to appear.

Dad was still very quiet, and even Tim, who did not always notice these things, had asked him what the matter was. But now it was Dad's turn to tell Tim to shut up.

For a while they fished in silence. There were not many other people around, just some little kids a few feet to the left of them who kept trying unsuccessfully to get their tilly lamp to work. Normally Dad would have gone and helped them. He was like that. But this time he didn't do anything and just sat staring at his rod.

'Now listen to me, lads. There's been a bit of trouble,' he said suddenly.

Sam felt an odd lurch in his stomach that suddenly became painful and Tim looked scared.

'What is it, Dad?' Tim looked like a trapped animal and Dad reached over to put his arm around him.

'It's all right, son. Nothing to get in a state about. I wanted to talk to you about young Wesley.'

'Wesley?' Sam stared up. 'What about him?'

'He's in a bit of trouble. Bad trouble.'

Sam still stared up, his face expressionless. Somewhere out at sea there was a mournful wail from the Goodwin lightship.

'He always was a right tearaway, that one,' said Dad.

'He's a good coach,' said Sam miserably. Something bad was coming. Then it came.

'He got a bit stoned and fell off a roof.' Dad paused.

'What roof?' asked Sam.

'Wineland.'

'But that's a big high roof,' put in Tim.

'Shut up,' said Sam, trying to kick him and missing.

'He's not too good.' Dad paused and then went on. 'In fact he's broken his back.'

Tim began to cry although he hardly knew Wes. Sam, who did, simply scowled.

'Was he on his own?' was all he could ask.

Dad shook his head. 'He had a mate with him. He went down in the shop. Nasty cuts and all but he'll be OK. It was Wes who copped it.'

'What's going to happen to him?' asked Sam. His voice was shaking.

'Well he's not going to croak or anything. But he might not walk again. We've got to face that.'

'Wes? Not walk?' Sam found this impossible to believe.

Dad said nothing and suddenly began to reel in his line. There was nothing on the end of it.

'What about football?' asked Sam miserably and then yelled at Tim. 'Stop crying, you baby.'

'He won't play football again,' said Dad. 'Most likely he'll be coaching it from a wheelchair.'

'It's not fair,' said Sam, suddenly beginning to cry quietly himself.

One of the little kids turned round and said to Colin:

'Mister, can you make our light work?'

'Course I can,' said Dad, leaning towards them. The gulls wheeled and cried out and Sam mourned Wes who would never kick a ball again.

It was a sad little fishing party that came home from Ramsgate that night. As they drove back in the failing light, Sam said:

'Were you there, Dad?'

'When, son?'

'When Wes fell off the roof.'

'Yeah.'

'Did you try to stop him?'

'You bet I did.'

'Thanks, Dad,' Sam said in an oddly passive voice.

When they got indoors Dad was tired and scratchy and Mum was in a hell of a bad mood. In fact she seemed to be absolutely furious in a way that Sam had never seen before and it frightened him. Tim seemed impervious to it all and ran upstairs to play with his snooker table. Trust him to duck out of trouble, thought Sam, but Mum was already in full flood and was yelling:

'You never told me nothing about Wesley.'

'I was going to.'

'You told the kids?'

'Yeah.'

'Typical. It's me who always gets to hear last.'

'Look, love . . . ' Dad looked tired and old as he tried unsuccessfully to reason with her.

'Don't "love" me. There's no love lost between you and me. There'll be hell to pay for this. You know what they're like – he's the apple of their eye, that boy. Although God knows why. He's one of the worst little sods round here and you've always encouraged him. Now you have to try and nick him and see what happens. Mark my words, after what I just learnt – and now this – there'll be trouble. A lot of trouble.'

Sam was suddenly speechless with anger. She was always moaning and now she was putting the boot in on Wes. But just as Sam was going to yell at her his dad turned and said:

'Hang on.'

And she did hang on, because it was rare that Dad raised his voice in the house and now he was raising it.

'You know who you're on about?' Colin asked her.

'I know who I'm on about.' But she was cowed now.

'You're talking about a kid who's not going to walk again. And don't give me one of your favourite phrases like "he deserves all he gets". I've known Wes since he was a kid . . . He's never stood a bleedin' chance. Not ever. And it's not right. He was a good kid but they never gave him a chance. He's a brilliant footballer and a good coach, or was. I could trust any kids with him. And yeah – I had to nick him, didn't I?' He paused. 'Anyway, where did you hear all this?'

'On LBC, wasn't it? And it'll be splashed all over the papers soon.' She stood by the tea table, literally wringing her hands, and it was this much-worn habit that finally seemed to incite Dad.

'I'm goin' down the boozer,' he muttered and walked straight out of the room. It was the last time Sam saw him.

Part Two
Mourning

'I shouldn't have spoken to him that way, son,' Mum said as she passed the boys their haddock and chips. Sam didn't answer and poured too much brown sauce over his plate. But for once Mum said nothing.

'What do you mean, Mum?' Tim's attention wandered back to Sam's plate. 'You've got too much sauce on there, Sam.'

'What do you want? A smack in the mouth?' Sam asked calmly, pouring even more sauce on to his plate. 'Or would you like me to push your teeth down the back of your throat?'

'I could beat you any day,' said Tim. 'You've been rotten to me all day.'

'Want to try it?' asked Sam but Mum intervened.

'Don't start, you two,' she said wearily. 'Things are bad enough, aren't they?' She looked over to the door, which Dad had so recently slammed behind him, and shivered. 'It's bad enough him being a copper without . . . ' When she realised that she was talking to herself she broke off and said:

'You're putting too much sauce on that fish, boy.' But Sam simply ignored her.

That evening Sam and Tim made it up and played a game of snooker. But all the time they played Sam could

15

not get Wes out of his mind. He was such a brilliant guy and Sam had always felt good when Wes had praised him, which wasn't very often because he was hard. But that was the way the boys in the team wanted him to be. They wanted him hard because he could teach them to play hard and that was what football was all about. Once some posh bloke had come along to talk to them at school. He'd been something to do with an FA training scheme and he'd had a real mouthful of potatoes. He kept telling them that football wasn't to do with winning, it was to do with team spirit. 'Rubbish to all that,' they had said afterwards. It wasn't that they didn't understand about playing as a team and sharing the ball and all that, because that made them win. It was the way he spoke.

'Sounds a right honky,' was Wes's verdict when they told him.

The possibility that Wes might be coaching from a wheelchair sounded almost horrific to Sam. He'd look such a wally, wouldn't he? Sam had met some kids in wheelchairs once when he had gone with the school to an adventure centre. The grown-ups had talked to them very loudly and brightly and there was a big bustling nurse who talked to the wheelchair kids as if they were deaf. It wasn't their fault. Dad would have spoken to them properly.

The proudest moment of Sam's life had been when his dad had come to talk at assembly. He had moved easily into the room and hadn't been nervous or patronising or any of those things. He had been Dad, but bigger than he remembered him. Sam had been dreading this visit ever since old Mrs Spittle-face had announced it the previous day. 'A visit from your very own community policeman,' she had gobbled at them like some old turkey and Sam had a fight in the playground with his best friend Jason because Jason had called his dad 'our very own community policeman'. Jason had duffed him up but it didn't matter because they were still mates. They were even better mates after Dad had spoken and Jason had whispered 'great guy' to him and even Tracey Anne had said: 'Isn't he a goer?' which was praise indeed. Dad had talked about not breaking the law and the highway code and speed and glue sniffing and not getting interfered with in the park. It was all old stuff but Dad had put it across brilliantly, with good jokes and a big plug for the team. He got a massive round of applause and Sam glowed with pride. When he had kissed him that night Sam had whispered 'You were great'. Dad had glowed with pride then.

About half-past nine Tim and Sam came down from their snooker game to watch the television. There was another copper in the hall and Sam recognised him as Jim Dowson, Dad's best mate. He was crying and telling Mum that Dad was dead.

During the next few days, Sam walked around as if he was in a dream. The house was continually full of people – relations, policemen and friends drinking innumerable cups of tea and glasses of sherry. Scrappy meals were occasionally set before him, but he felt totally numb and Tim and Mum seemed to drift round him like ghosts. He could feel no contact with them, neither could he sense that they were trying to reach him. Most of the time Sam spent outside the house, wandering the streets and riding the tube. When she could think of it, Mum gave him money so that he could amuse himself. She made no attempt to keep him in. In fact she made no attempt to communicate with him at all;

their nan was looking after Tim. All Mum could do was sob or drink or go on talking endlessly to the relatives.

Strangely, once he was on the streets, Sam found he could reach Dad, and when he was walking along, felt his hand inside his own. But once he was back in the house, Dad simply disappeared, so Sam spent as much time as he could outside. Hand in hand with Dad he would ride the tubes, and the only thing he kept noticing was how dirty everything was. The carriage floor seemed ankle-deep in debris, cartons dribbling chips and stale hamburgers, and old coke cans which kept rolling across as the tube rattled and roared through the tunnels. Most of the seats seemed either ripped or broken.

Outside in the streets there were torn dustbin bags leaking smelly refuse and most of the paving tiles were cracked or broken. London was a dump and he had never noticed it before. Neither had he really noticed all the big kids hanging around on the street corners and the graffiti on every wall. Most of the shops had steel shutters and lots of the windows on the big estates were boarded up. But whilst he was outside, Sam was with Dad and that was all he needed. He still couldn't feel anything. Only the remembered warmth of Dad's hand.

At home, Sam could feel no sense of time at all. Mum had said they needn't go to school – not till after the funeral anyway – and Sam still had no idea when that was. Quite often he would hear Mum's voice in the front room as she raged against 'them' and what 'they' had done to Dad. Something had happened when Dad was in the pub. 'They' had hurt him in some way that Sam did not want to know.

18

When he wasn't riding the tube or wandering the streets, Sam went into amusement arcades and played the machines. Dad was kind of hovering in these places but he wasn't really there. As Sam gazed into a video game called UNDERSEA BATTLE WORLD he could see the seaweed-hung gantries and galleries under Ramsgate pier rather than the computer graphics. He could see Dad sitting and fixing the little kids' tilly lamp, and through the bleeps and buzzing he could hear them say: 'Mister, can you make our light work?'

A couple of days after it had all happened, Sam found himself outside a place that had always terrified him. Normally he avoided it but in his numbness he had arrived at the very door.

The Tivoli was an old cinema that had once been a bingo hall and was now a dilapidated venue for rock concerts. It was a huge barn of a place and with its sooty brickwork and rusty canopy it had the appearance of a medieval fortress. A few tatty, gaudy posters adorned its walls and pale neon lighting only served to heighten the impression of fortified gloom. As if this was not enough, Sam saw to his horror that standing on the steps was Albino Man, with his livid white features. Dad had said he was harmless enough, but when Sam sought for the warm memory of his dad's hand, it was no longer there and he was clutching at damp air. Then, as if from a long distance, he heard Dad's voice saying: 'Don't worry, son. He's only an old man. He's harmless enough.' But the voice was very faint and distant.

'Hallo, Sam.' The voice was old and strangely cracked, and his dirty white teeth shone mysteriously in the pale oval of his face.

Sam paused, wishing he could run away, but his legs were wooden and heavy. Albino Man was the manager of the Tivoli, and according to Mum never did a hand's turn to keep the place clean. Dad had told him the old cinema was owned by a property developer who was waiting for Albino Man's lease to run out before tearing it down to build a shopping precinct. But Albino Man's image, much embroidered at school, was of a monster who killed children. The more Dad had tried to stop the story spreading, the more Sam and his friends elaborated on it. It was good to feel terrified as a group of mates, but it was awful to feel scared in your dreams. And now here was Albino Man actually walking down the steps towards him, one strangely pigmented hand outstretched.

'I'm sorry about your dad, Sam. Real sorry. He was a good man.'

Sam felt Albino Man's hand on his arm and cried out in fear and a kind of rage that he should be handled. Suddenly Sam found the strength to run and he ran and ran, skidding over the pavement so fast that he thought his feet weren't touching the ground. And behind him he could hear Albino Man running in his funny horrible light way but when he turned round he was still standing on the steps of the Tivoli. Sam stopped and turned again. No longer frightened, he was suddenly in the worst rage of his life. Albino Man had made him run away from Dad and he had left Dad behind. Forever. He could no longer sense Dad's hand or his voice. He was gone. Dead. And Albino Man had done it.

Sam stood in the centre of the cracked pavement and yelled all the abuse he could think of at the old man standing on the steps of the cinema. But Albino Man simply waved back.

The funeral was awful, but at least Sam cried. They all cried, although it would be fairer to say that Tim howled. He clung on to Sam with such ferocity that Sam almost hit him, and then thought better of it. The three of them stood by the graveside, looking down at the coffin. It was not possible to believe that Dad was inside. It looked too small anyway and for a horrible moment Sam wondered whether they had broken his legs to get him in. He had read about that somewhere, or was it on a video? There was a massive escort with policemen marching in a line behind the funeral hearse, and in the church, four burly officers carried the coffin. As Sam sat there in the pew he trembled with a combination of fear and pride and loss. They had lost the best dad in all the world, but there were so many people who had thought well of him. The church was packed, and after the funeral there was a reception at home organised by one of his aunties. Ada was 'good' at funerals. She had buried her parents and a husband and knew that mourners expected meat sandwiches, fairy cakes, strong tea and ale and sherry. She had laid on mounds of stuff and, guiltily, Sam found that he was ravenously hungry. Tim had quietened down and seemed in a daze, sucking his thumb on his nan's lap. Sam wondered if he was going to see it all through by becoming a baby again. Mum looked drunk, which she was a bit, and was telling a group of consoling policemen's wives about how she first met Dad at a Rock and Roll concert. Most of the men were in the kitchen and Sam could hear their subdued voices and the glugging of beer from a barrel.

The postman walked briskly up the path with the afternoon post and Sam went to the door. To his surprise there was a letter addressed to him and he quickly tore it open.

Dear Sam,

Sorry about your dad. He was a good bloke even if he did nick me. I'm in Streatham General. Roberts Ward. I feel lousy. Come in and see me soon.

　　　　　Yours,
　　　　　　Wes

After a long time, most of the mourners left and Mum went up to bed with a retinue of aunties to watch over her. The doctor had given her some pills to make her sleep. Tim and Sam sat watching television with their nan. She was Dad's mum and she was a very strong person. She had cried with the rest of them but Sam knew that she was thinking of them now and not so much of Dad. It warmed him to have her around. Tim still seemed dazed and his hand kept slipping into Sam's as they watched *Dallas*. Sam didn't have the heart to push it away.

When the programme was over, Sam showed Nan Wes's letter. She lived in Wimbledon so it was some time before she reacted to his name. Eventually Nan sat back and kind of snorted. Then she said brusquely:

'You can't go there.'

'Why not?'

She paused and Sam saw that she was looking at him very seriously. In fact she seemed to be weighing him up. Then she stood up and grasped Tim's hand.

'Come along, Tim. It's bedtime. I'll talk to you in a minute, Sam.'

She dragged off a protesting Tim and Sam turned off the TV. What on earth did she want to talk to him about?

Nan came back into the room with two big steaming cups of cocoa. She was the only one who could make such lovely stuff. It was thick and strong and really tasted of chocolate.

'Your dad was one of the best,' she said as she sat down heavily. 'And I'm going to tell you something that your dear mum wouldn't want me to tell you. But I have to. Now that boy has written, though I'd've wanted to – even if he hadn't.'

'Wes?'

'Yes.' She paused and stirred her cocoa carefully. 'You're bound to find this out sooner or later so I might as well tell you now. Your mum's in no fit state to tell you.' She paused again. 'Your mum and dad didn't always get on that well. No one's fault. So your dad had a friend. And he had that friend for many years. Long before you were born. And they kept their friendship a very big secret. I knew, and a few days ago your mum knew who it was. She's a strange woman, your mum. She feels she can't get close to anyone. And because she feels she can't, she doesn't. See what I mean?'

Sam nodded. He did see what she meant.

'Anyway, your dad and his friend went on seeing each other. She was on her own and she knew there was no future in it. I don't think that worried her. But it worried her brother. He'd been away for years, but when he got home recently he heard what was going on and began to stir up trouble. And there was plenty to stir up. After all, your dad was a neighbourhood policeman and the lady in question – well, she was black.'

She paused, wondering if Sam was going to say anything, perhaps giving him the opportunity. But he simply stared back at her with no expression on his face at all.

'Of course they'd always been very careful. They never met in this area. They had what your dad called a 'safe house' in Wimbledon. Near me. They loved each other very much for a very long time. And what a secret to keep! I mean if the blacks round here had found out, there would have been hell to pay. Absolute hell. A copper going round with a black woman. You can imagine . . . '

Sam could imagine.

'Did you know her?' he said in a thin voice.

'A little. I liked her very much.'

'What did Mum say when she found out?'

'Not a lot. She was very depressed and frightened, poor soul.' Nan smiled very sadly down at him. 'Now you won't go thinking ill of your dad, will you?'

'Course not.'

'He was only human, like the rest of us. I won't say the situation was a good one. But it was there, that's all.'

'And this brother –'

'He didn't find out until recently. He'd been back in Jamaica for years.'

Sam suddenly sat up. 'You mean –'

She nodded. 'Your dad was in the pub when her brother came in. There was a fight and your dad slipped and hit his head.'

'He didn't mean to kill him – this man?'

'I don't think so. Anyway he's scarpered. The police are looking for him.'

'I didn't hear about a black man killing him.'

'It wasn't just the black man and your dad in a fight – there were white men too.'

'What were they fighting him for?' Suddenly it seemed as if the whole world had been against his dad.

Nan saw the tears he was trying to hold back and drew him to her. He sat on the floor with his head on her knee.

'It's all a bit of a muddle. I think your dad ran across some villains and they started and the black man started and everybody started. It was all a mess. No one's very clear about anything.'

'Is there anything else?' Sam was trembling.

His nan sighed, wondering if she was making everything so much worse. But what was the right thing to do?'

'Yes. This boy. Wes. The kid your dad helped so much. He was the black man's son. Your dad's friend is Wes's aunt.'

For a while Sam gazed at her uncomprehendingly, then he shrugged his shoulders angrily. 'Don't you know? Dad nicked him and he fell off a roof and broke –'

'I know all about that. But you've got to understand. Wes's dad is on the run. He didn't just want to get your dad because of his sister. He wanted to get him for Wes too. And if you see Wes, well – it makes it all the more complicated and dangerous. He's a bad lot that boy and his father's no better.'

'Does Wes know about Dad carrying on with his auntie?'

'They were so secret.' Nan suddenly sounded as if she was talking to herself. 'I've never known such a secret. But Wes knows now OK. And he's going to use it. And you.'

'How?'

'How do I know? But I'm sure he will.'

Sam got up.

'Where are you going, son?'

'Bed. I'm knackered.'

'I had to tell you. You're not to think bad of your dad. He was human. Like everyone else.'

Sam suddenly stopped in the doorway.

'Nan –'

'Yes, my darling?'

'If Dad's friend was Wes's auntie, doesn't it make me and Wes kind of cousins?'

She smiled and shook her head.

Sam frowned. 'I think we are,' he said firmly. 'Wes and me.'

He went out of the room and his nan watched him go uneasily.

Sam hardly slept that night, and when he did he had a succession of such appalling nightmares that he immediately woke again. Once again Albino Man dominated his dreams, but they were further confused by aunts and cousins and Nan, aunts and cousins who were not really his own, all engaged in a snowball fight on the common. There was plenty of snow but it also seemed to be midsummer and the sun was dazzling in its brightness and heat. But the snow didn't melt and he saw Tim stuck up a tree. He kept calling for help but no one listened to him except Sam who told him to shut up. Mum wasn't in the dream at all but Dad was. He and Wes suddenly ran on with the football team, ploughing up the snow in feathery flakes. Sam saw that he had his own football kit on and Dad kept yelling at him to play right attack. But there were no opponents, and when Sam asked Dad who they were playing he laughed and said the wind. And the wind did play with them, tossing the ball here and there. That was the only good part of the dream.

But then, as they rushed through the snow, the flakes stirred under their feet and rose up as gulls who flew wheeling and mewing into the sky and somewhere ahead Sam saw the sea. Up in the trees, Tim still cried for help but everyone ignored him. Then the wind stopped playing with them and another team ran on to the field. They were all black and were entirely composed of aunts

26

and cousins. Up in the tree with Tim, Sam saw Albino Man. Tim was dead and Albino Man was eating his heart. 'They don't belong to you,' he shouted down at Sam, and all the aunts and cousins laughed and ran away over the common.

'Now we've got no team to play against,' shouted Wes, and Albino Man threw Tim's head down on to the pitch.

'Play with that,' he yelled and they did.

Sam scored a goal with Tim's head and looked across to the touchline to see if Dad was cheering. But he wasn't there and in his place was an open grave.

Sam woke up sweating and cried alone for his dad into the grey dawn. Later he slept and no longer dreamed. He woke refreshed and with an odd little glow of comfort from somewhere he could not define. Then he thought of Wes's aunt and Wes, the cousin that did not really belong to him. They were a part of Dad's life that he did not know. He suddenly made a resolution: he would explore the bits of Dad's life that he didn't know and find the bits of Dad he didn't know either. Sam turned over and slept.

Part Three
The Journey

When Sam awoke he knew immediately what he had to do. It was nine but the whole house was quiet. He crept out of his room and listened; nothing stirred. They were all so tired after the funeral that they must all be still asleep. He crept down into the kitchen and left a note for his nan on the kitchen table. Then he hurried out of the house.

Sam arrived at Streatham Hill General just after nine. It was a forbidding-looking building at the best of times, but now a light grey drizzle gave the sprawling building an unpleasant greasy sheen. Sam walked into the reception area which smelt of a mixture of antiseptic and coffee with the milk gone off.

Seeing a sign pointing to Roberts Ward, Sam followed it through a gloomy corridor. When he got to the ward he paused by the rubber doors and pushed his way in. Immediately a nurse blocked his way. She had a huge bosom and the suggestion of a black moustache.

'Where do you think you are going?' she began unhelpfully, looking at Sam as if he were an insect.

'I've come to see a friend.'

'You should be in school.'

'My dad died. I don't have to go back till next week.'

'Oh.' She seemed surprised. 'These aren't visiting hours, you know.'

'I've got to go back and look after my mum,' said Sam calculatingly. It seemed to work and he saw a little bead of sweat begin to form on her lip. Got her on the run, he thought.

'Who do you want to see?'

'Wes. Wesley. I can't remember his other name.'

'I know Wesley.' She stared down at Sam as if she was trying to connect him with something and failed. 'You a relation?'

'I'm his cousin.'

She paused, trying to make a decision, and then one of the nurses called her from deep within the ward.

'Sister. Mr Wold's done it again.'

Sister's face tightened in grim fury at the news. 'You can see him for ten minutes,' she snapped as she stumped away.

Wesley was lying on his back in a kind of harness, reading a comic through a mirror. His face was bandaged and Sam could see that both his eyes were swollen.

'Wes.'

He looked up and almost seemed afraid. 'Sam.'

'Thought I'd see how you were.'

'Get my note – it was painful to write.'

'Yeah.'

'I'm sorry.'

'Yeah.'

'Did they let you in all right?'

'I said I was your cousin. She's not nice.'

'Sister? A right cow.'

There was a long silence. Then Wes said: 'Lloyd really copped it.'

'How is he?' Sam knew Lloyd. He'd come to the football a couple of times. He was a nice guy. Very jokey.

29

'Fractured skull. Two broken arms. But he'll walk again. You'll see.'

There was another long silence and Sam could feel Wes's bitterness like a wall between them.

'How's it going?' asked Wes very softly.

'All right.'

'I got somethin' to tell you.' There was a sudden urgency in his voice.

'What?'

'Come closer.'

Sam edged closer to Wes, who looked more like some kind of semi-human machine than a boy. Sam wondered if he knew that he would never walk again. Then he was sure that he did.

'Your mum.'

'Yeah?'

'She knows something she didn't oughta.'

Sam stared at him. 'What does she know?'

'Something she shouldn't.'

'I don't know what you mean.' Sam was suddenly on the edge of tears.

Wes looked impatient, but suddenly his face screwed up in pain and he began to whimper.

'Shall I call the nurse?' asked Sam, forgetting his tears.

Wes shook his head. 'I need a shot. But she'll only chuck you out. I'll have to be quick. It's a stitch up.'

'Eh?'

The pain surged through Wes again and Sam decided that he'd better keep quiet, even if he didn't understand a word of what Wes was on about.

'Listen. The Old Bill reckon my dad did your dad in. It's not true. He wants to make it look like that.'

'He?' asked Sam, forgetting his resolution.

'Uncle George. He wants to pin it on us lot. Us blacks. My dad never did nothing. He was angry, see. 'Bout me and everything else. But he wouldn't have touched him. Not that way. It's too dodgy. He'd have tried to stir up trouble. But not kill a copper. He didn't do it. On my mother's life.'

The torrent of words made Sam feel sick. 'Who's Uncle George?' he choked.

'Your mum knows who he is. Your dad told her. And he'll get her. And make it look like it was my dad again.'

'Where's your dad?'

'Done a runner, hasn't he.'

'But if my mum knows who these guys are, why doesn't she tell the police?'

'She's scared. That's why.' Wes squirmed and let out a hoarse cry of pain. 'It's time for my shot,' he whimpered, gripping the sheet so hard that Sam could see his whitened knuckles. 'Albino Man,' he muttered. 'He'll help you.'

'Him?'

But the big nurse was there, bustling away. 'All right, young man. Out you go.'

Wes suddenly winked. 'She's a right fascist.'

'None of your cheek, Wesley.' She advanced on him with a needle, snarling at Sam. 'Go on. Hoppit.'

For the next few days, Sam resumed his wanderings, while Wesley's words drummed in his mind relentlessly. Sometimes he thought about them so much that he began to confuse all the names. He spent the last day before he went back to school in a state of increasing panic. Sometimes he wanted to go back to Wesley so they could talk again, but he lacked the courage to face the Sister and the pain that was in Wesley's eyes.

Most of the visitors at home had now departed but his nan stayed – she seemed almost to have replaced Mum, who now seemed frightened, wary. He knew why but being Mum he couldn't bring himself to talk to her about it as he could have with Dad. She kept to her bed and only came down in the afternoon in her dressing-gown to gawp dazedly at the TV. Tim now ran to Nan instead of Mum. There seemed to be nothing more to say. She was like a frightened ghost as she drifted hopelessly round the house. Sam was almost angry. He just couldn't understand why what had happened hadn't changed her. After all, she was meant to be comforting them, or was she expecting something from him?

As for Sam's journeys with Dad, he was simply no longer with him and this was the hardest part to bear. It was as if Albino Man had captured his spirit, and although Sam often darted past the cinema in the hope that he could pick up where he left off, there was no sign of Dad's return. In the evenings he would watch the television with Tim under the watchful eye of Nan, and then he would go to bed and try to dream about Dad. But no dreams would come. Oddly enough, Sam would even have welcomed a nightmare in case he saw Dad – even in a bad moment. But at least he slept. Sam was now ready and even looking forward to school, although he was dreading all the questions the other kids were bound to ask.

In fact everyone welcomed him back in a very ordinary way and he was pleased to see Jason. The Head called Sam into his office. 'We're very pleased to see you again, Sam,' he said, 'and I just wanted to say one or two things.' Sam braced himself for the attack. Mr Potter was young and friendly but Sam found him too serious. He was always talking about counselling and deprivation. But this morning he seemed more normal somehow.

'We're very proud of your dad here. He's a hero to all of us and we would like you to know that.' He cleared his throat and looked out of the window across the playground as Sam stood silently in front of him.

'There was a time when we didn't have community policemen walking round on their beat, chatting to people.' He paused again. 'There was a time when the police crawled around in cars, completely anonymous and perhaps too frightened to get out. You see, it needs courage to walk these streets. You know that, Sam. And your dad had courage all right. But he had more than that. He had humanity. That's all I'm going to say. Except that he will also be sorely missed on the football field. But you know that better than I do. Yes?'

Sam nodded and Mr Potter looked at him anxiously, wondering if he had gone too far and Sam was going to cry. But Sam didn't feel like crying. Instead he felt all warm inside and almost shaking with sudden excitement. My dad's a hero, he thought. He had never seen him in that light. Wait till he got home and told Tim.

Later on in the playground, Jason and all his other mates stood round him and, instead of kicking a ball about, they all wanted to talk. At least they wanted Sam to talk and for once they were prepared to listen. They kept asking him questions about Dad's job and what he was like at home and what was going to happen to the team and how Wes was. But they never mentioned how Dad had died or who had killed him. Sam talked and talked through break and then through lunch break and no one seemed to get bored. The only thing he didn't tell them about were the fishing expeditions. They were private. Also Sam felt that if he could only get back to Ramsgate pier, he might see Dad again. And if he shared the memory with anyone, Dad would disappear from the pier as well.

That night, Sam walked home contented. Momentarily, his grief was forgotten and he could bask in the warmth of his father's reputation. He wanted to tell Tim and Nan what the kids and Mr Potter had been saying about Dad. He never even thought of including his mum.

Sam took a short cut over the rec to his house. Usually he walked home with Jason, but he had got to go to a music lesson. The rec was a rather grubby open space with an ornamental bandstand that had fallen into disrepair, a couple of football pitches on which they had often played league matches, and a boarded-up pavilion covered in graffiti. It was still raining gently and was so dull that at a quarter-past four the night was stealing softly over the ragged grass, cloaking the pavilion in all kinds of strange shadows. As for the bandstand, it looked like a gingerbread cottage standing in the clearing of some deep forest.

As he passed the bandstand Sam saw a sudden movement. So preoccupied was he with his thoughts that he called out softly, 'Dad?' There was no reply, yet the shadows moved again. But with Dad so much in his mind, Sam wasn't afraid. He stared into the dark thicket of broken chairs and wooden spars and saw the movement again. Slowly he began to walk past the bandstand, whilst still staring into its depths.

Then Sam saw movement again and two shapes detached themselves. For a moment the shapes looked like a man and a child, and for a crazy moment he imagined he was watching Dad and Tim. But the tall shape was much leaner than Dad, and the other was chubbier, rounder and taller than Tim. Suddenly, Sam

34

felt himself grabbed by the neck and thrown to the ground. A match flared and in its pallid light he saw the livid features of a boy with a Mohican haircut. Part of his pale head was shaved and he wore a Union Jack T-shirt. Then the match fizzled out and Sam was left panting in the darkness.

'Don't move,' said the Mohican boy, and in the wan moonlight Sam saw a big pair of Doc Marten boots that were scuffed and stained as if they had been well used for more than walking. The boots nudged at Sam and he rolled fearfully on to his back. His heart was pounding and he felt tears jerking at the back of his eyelids. The boot nudged him again and a gutteral voice said:

'You move and you're dead.'

Sam didn't move and the Mohican boy bent down. Then, rather slowly and cautiously, he knelt down beside him. The other figure remained stationary, staring down.

'I'll get my dad on you,' said Sam, hardly realising what he was saying. But the boy laughed and punched him on the arm. Sam whimpered. It hurt and the sound that he made reminded him of Wes.

'Your dad's croaked.'

Sam said nothing.

'Croaked.'

Still he said nothing and the boy punched him on his arm again. This time it hurt more.

'He's dead. Copped it.' The boy laughed at the pun. 'Eh?'

'Yeah.'

'I took a walk round your place this afternoon.'

Immediately Sam was afraid. Very afraid.

'Why?'

'I had business. Business with your mum.'

'Mum?'

'But she weren't there, was she?'

Sam stared at him amazed. Anyway what did this bastard want with her? Sam began to tremble and stiffened his body, trying to conceal the shaking.

'She weren't there when I wanted her.' He prodded at Sam with a thin jeaned knee. It was so sharp that it looked like a cruel beak.

'I don't know what you want.'

'Your mum's gone away.'

'Gone away? Who told you?'

'An old girl.'

'My nan.'

'Maybe.'

'She hasn't —' Sam stopped talking. It was obviously best to say nothing. Nothing at all.

'What was you gonna say?'

'Nothing.'

Again he punched Sam on the arm with an uncanny instinct for where there was already a bruise. Sam winced but he was determined not to cry. For a moment he wondered if he could break and run, but it would mean fighting and he was outnumbered. So he stayed still, praying that someone would come but no one did.

'Where is she?'

'Nowhere.'

Another punch and this one hurt so badly that Sam writhed in agony.

'There's plenty more where that came from if you don't tell me where she is.'

'She was at home.'

'She ain't now.'

'Then I don't know.'

Another punch and this time Sam broke down and sobbed. The Mohican boy grabbed him by the shoulders and shook him, hauling Sam to his feet.

'Know who this is?' He gestured angrily behind him. He lit a match and the light flared into a black face. It was a boy – a West Indian boy – of about Sam's age. 'Know who he is?' repeated the Mohican.

'No.'

'He's your bleedin' brother, isn't he?'

'Brother?'

'Yeah.'

Sam was completely bewildered and still trembling. He could think of nothing to say and there was nothing in his mind either.

'Listen. And listen good. His uncle did in your old man. And now he's done a runner. And this kid's mum is your dad's bit. Right?' Sam shook his head.

'And what I'm doing is trying to protect your mum.'

Sam felt the Mohican boy grinning in the dark.

'You – protect my mum?' Sam almost laughed.

'Against the coons. You see – she knows a few names and a few addresses passed on by your dad. That's only natural, isn't it? And the coons want the message. They want what she knows. See?' But he didn't wait for Sam to reply. 'The coons,' he said slowly, 'they're mean. Winston here can tell you that. They're real mean. Your mum knows a bloody sight too much and they aim to shut her up. Right, Winston?'

But the black boy did not reply.

'And I want to warn her, like. But I can't if I don't know where she is. Can I?'

Sam knew instinctively that the Mohican boy was lying, that he could not trust him. But if Mum really wasn't at the house, where was she? Suddenly Sam realised that

37

Nan must have been lying. Mum *was* in the house – and in danger.

'Help!' yelled Sam very suddenly and very loudly. 'Someone help me!' For a moment the Mohican boy looked disconcerted and Sam took his chance to bellow again. Meanwhile Winston stood very still.

'You shut up.' The Mohican boy raised his hand and slapped Sam round the head. The pain was almost blinding and the stinging sensation was coupled with a tearing feeling. Sam knew he had been cut and that his cheek was bleeding. The boy must be wearing a ring.

'Leave me alone,' Sam pleaded.

'Where's your mum?' The boy began to advance on Sam and he knew that he was now more afraid then he had ever been in his life. 'Want another one?'

'Leave me alone.' Sam looked round desperately but there was no one there and it was only a waste of breath calling for help. But he called again and again until his breath ran out and he collapsed in great shuddering sobs. And still the Mohican boy advanced and raised his hand as Sam began to back away.

'Where is she?'

'I don't know.'

Still the Mohican boy advanced, his hand now bunched into a fist. Anger welled up in Sam, replacing all the fear and terror and apprehension. He stood his ground, his own fists bunched as the Mohican boy came within inches of him.

'Don't come near me,' Sam yelled.

The Mohican boy sniggered. Then from behind him something moved. Something threw itself at him. The silent Winston leapt and grabbed the Mohican boy round the neck. For a moment he swayed and then fell to the

38

ground, with Winston on top. Sam did not hesitate as he threw himself on the struggling heap.

It was the worst and most terrifying fight that Sam had ever been in. But his temper was up and he was like a snarling animal, hardly conscious of the blows he received. The three of them rolled over and over on the ground, scratching, slashing, biting, kicking, tearing and punching. Winston used his head several times to butt at the taller boy and draw blood from his nose and mouth. Still they rolled and threshed on the wet and muddy ground and Sam thought that it was never going to end.

Then Winston's head butted again and the tall boy stopped struggling. He lay on the ground with blood flowing from his mouth and his head. He was still.

For a moment Sam lay on the grass beside him, coughing and wheezing and gasping. He heard Winston breathing hard beside him and eventually he gasped out: 'We got to go, man.'

'Where?' asked Sam stupidly, but he could feel Winston's hand on his arm, trying to drag him to his feet. For a moment he resisted and then staggered up. 'Where we going?'

'Anywhere. Away from here. Can you run?'

'OK.'

And they began to limp and then run as fast as they could. As they tore round the back of the pavilion, Sam realised that he was running in the opposite direction to home. He stopped short and paused, panting, with his hands on his knees.

'Wait.'

'Come on, man. He'll be on his feet in a minute.'

'I'm going the wrong way.'

'We should go towards the lights.'

Sam realised that Winston was right, and they sped on until their feet touched tarmac and they were on the path that led to the lighted road. Opposite them was Safeway. They dashed inside and took refuge by a huge pile of toilet rolls.

'Who are you?' asked Sam when he had regained some breath. Now that he could see him, Winston was just a little bit taller than him and was stockily built, with big shoulders and a scar on his cheek.

'He was right. I *am* your brother. Or at least half-brother, maybe.'

Sam looked at him incredulously.

'Your auntie . . . ' he began, 'and my dad.' He paused in total confusion and Winston suddenly laughed.

'She is Wes's auntie and my mum.'

Sam shook his head.

'They were together a long time. At least,' Winston corrected himself, 'they were going with each other a long time.'

'Who?'

'You thick or somethin'?'

Sam shook his head again. Then he said: 'Why didn't I ever know?'

'Best kept secret since sliced bread.'

'But you weren't at the – at the funeral.'

'I told you. It was a best kept secret.'

'So why are you here now?'

'Alfie – that skinny bastard – grabbed me.'

'Who is Uncle George?'

'He's a right villain. Dad was on to him.'

Sam looked round and saw that one of the managers was advancing on him. Then he saw someone else.

'Blimey.'

'What?' Winston whipped round. It was Alfie and he had seen them. Soiled and bloody, he was advancing on them. And advancing on him was the manager.

'Bunk,' said Winston. They bolted off down the length of the supermarket away from the checkouts. As they ran, Winston suddenly yelled:

'Keep together.'

'OK.'

'Go for the emergency exit.'

'Right.'

Alfie was gaining on them, charging round the shelves and scattering a huge pile of cans. The shoppers watched the chase with interest and no one stopped them. Alfie seemed impervious to the shouting manager who was being left behind. He was still gaining on Sam and Winston, his gaze fixed on Sam.

Alfie cut a very strange figure. His Union Jack T-shirt was ripped to shreds, his jeans were torn, his close-cropped skull was matted with mud and his face was bloody. He looked rather like a spindly, broken-down Action Man.

Suddenly Sam saw an old lady in front of them. She was pushing a trolley, trying to use it as a battering ram, but they dodged her easily.

'Vandals,' she yelled, 'I know your sort. You shout things through my letterbox. Vandals,' she yelled again, getting more skilful with her battering ram, as Alfie bore down on her. She threw the trolley at him and it caught Alfie in the midriff, winding him and sending him sprawling on the floor. As Sam looked back from the Emergency Exit he saw Alfie's thin legs kicking, the manager closing in and the old lady standing by her upturned trolley yelling:

'That'll teach you to shout things through my letterbox.'

'Who is she?' asked Sam as they ran out into the backstreet.

'An angel of God,' replied Winston.

Round the back of the supermarket was a used car lot and a garage forecourt. Sam and Winston ran across the light and disappeared into a road full of fading Victorian houses. Abandoned cars littered the streets and many of the houses were painted in bright colours. Television sets flickered from behind drawn curtains and booming, beating music resounded from behind one door. At the end of the street, they paused, panting, and looked behind them to see if they were being followed. There was no one. They stopped and leant against a crumbling garden wall.

'I've got to get back,' said Winston.

'Where do you live?'

'It would be best if I didn't tell you,' he said, almost in a whisper.

'I want to see you again.'

'Not yet.'

Sam looked at Winston and again felt a sense of yearning for the parts of Dad's life that he had never known. Winston – and his mum – could tell him things he didn't know. And that way, Dad and he would be able to walk through the streets hand in hand again.

'I must see you again,' said Sam urgently. 'And why can't I meet your mum?'

Winston looked scared. 'It would make you unhappy. It wouldn't be right.'

'It would make me happy,' said Sam firmly. 'You're part of me. And Dad.'

Winston was silent. 'I know where you live,' he said eventually. 'I know where you go to school. I'll contact you.'

'But doesn't Uncle George know too? And Alfie? And after what we've done to Alfie . . . '

'We can look after ourselves,' said Winston fiercely and turned away. He began to run off.

'When shall I see you again?' called Sam desperately.

But Winston sped on and did not reply. Sam watched his stocky, determined figure disappear around the corner.

'Where's Mum?'

'Come in, love, and I'll tell you.'

Nan looked her usual reassuring self as she stood on the doorstep. Inside, Tim was singing along with a television pop show. As Sam came through the door, Nan took one look at his face and clothes and cried out:

'What's happened?'

'Got into a fight, didn't I?'

'What about?'

'Nothing.'

'Your face is scratched to bits and you've got a black eye coming.'

'Thanks.'

'And your clothes. Your mum will kill you. Look at that sweater. It's ripped right across the shoulder. And your jeans . . . ' She broke off and Sam repeated:

'Where's Mum?'

'She's gone away for a few days, love. Down to Auntie Sue at Hastings. Just to have a rest.'

'Is that the only reason?'

His nan stared at him hard.

'Of course.'

'Did someone come round to see her today.'

She paused. 'Well yes. Some berk. Skinhead.'

'What did he say?'

'Wanted to see her. I sent him packing. God knows who he was.' She looked guilty and uneasy. Sam looked up at her and knew that she was telling the truth. 'Anyway your mum needs the rest. You don't mind me looking after you? Tim doesn't.' Her voice quavered suddenly and he realised how tired she must be.

Sam reached up and they hugged each other. 'Course not,' he said. What had Mum been doing for them anyway?

'Sam.' There was a sharp note in her voice.

'Yeah?'

'This fight.'

'Hang on,' he said as he ran upstairs to the bathroom. 'I'll go and have a bath. Tell you after.'

He would at least have time to make something up.

'You been in a fight?'

'Shut up.'

'Who won?'

'Shut up.'

Sam lay on the sofa and picked up a comic, shutting out the sight of Tim's curious face.

'It was good at school today,' said Tim.

'Mm.'

'Everyone said what a great guy Dad was.'

Sam put down his comic and grinned at Tim. 'Same here. It was brilliant.'

'Dad's a hero,' pronounced Tim.

'He is.'

Sam picked up his comic again. Then he put it down and glanced at Tim, sprawled on the floor below him. He looked awfully young.

'Hey, Tim – do you want a game of snooker?'

Later on Sam told his nan that he had got into a fight with Jason over nothing and that he didn't want to talk about it. It was unfair to Jason, but it was the only thing he could think of. His nan seemed to accept the lame explanation. Perhaps she was too tired not to.

Towards bedtime, Sam went to put the milk bottles out and he looked up and down the road. He was afraid. What if Alfie was prowling about, bent on revenge? What if the mysterious Uncle George was walking towards the house? Sam wondered what he would look like. He saw in his mind's eye a bulky figure in an astrakhan coat with a cigar. Then the image faded and Sam slammed the door. As he did so, he remembered what Wes had told him about Albino Man, and how he could help. But how could *he* help? Albino Man, of all people.

Sam kissed Nan goodnight and trooped wearily upstairs to bed. He felt desperately tired and very stiff. His whole body seemed to be aching and he fell on his bed with a great sense of unreality. He was so tired that he seemed to be drifting and when Nan came up to tuck him in and dress his cuts and do something about his eye, he was fast asleep. She stood staring down at the battered innocence of his face and silently began to cry. 'Oh, Colin,' she said inside herself. 'Oh, my dear Colin, our little boy is streetwise now all right.'

Sam woke at about three in the morning. He was shivering and despite the blankets and an eiderdown heaped over him he felt desperately cold. He tried to turn over and burrow further into the bedclothes but the more he tried the more cold he felt. He struggled out of bed and, still shivering, went over to his electric fire and turned it on. Then he stiffened and went to the window. He was sure he'd heard a noise outside in the street. Sam twitched open the curtains and stared down. It was a brilliant night and the whole street was picked out in icy silhouette.

The figures were crouched by his own doorway. Sam watched them hypnotically as they fiddled with something in the winking cold. Then he heard a grunt of satisfaction as they slipped a package through the letter box. There were two of them. They moved back and one of them reached into a bag and pulled out some kind of cylindrical object. With great force he hurled it through the window.

At the crash of breaking glass Sam's violent shivering increased and panic surged through his body as he watched the two figures run down the street and disappear round the corner. A sound that he could not immediately identify beat in his ears. It was a loud crackle of flames.

Sam's first thought was for Nan and Tim and he rushed into his little brother's room first and shook him awake. Tim kept turning over, but he finally surfaced when Sam had bellowed into his ear for the fifth time that the house was on fire. Now Tim was beside him, shivering and clutching at Sam in fear. They both ran into Nan's room but she was as difficult to rouse as Tim had been. Eventually they managed to wake her and soon all three were standing on the landing. Below them a mass of searing, red flames leapt and danced. The three of them ran back into Nan's bedroom and dashed to the window. The street looked an awful long way down but thankfully it was no longer deserted. Lights were coming up in some of the houses and already people were standing on the pavement, staring at the flames like zombies.

Nan pulled open the window and yelled at them: 'Someone get a ladder.'

A man darted back into his house, but already Sam could smell the acrid smoke below them. It was billowing up the stairs and the first wisps were coming in at the door. The smell was horrible and Tim began to cry. Nan meanwhile was leaning over the edge of the windowsill and yelling down to the street in a matter-of-fact voice. Despite the smoke, Tim stopped crying, reassured.

'The fire brigade, Mrs Hodgson. Have you called them?'

Mrs Hodgson yelled back indistinctly but Nan heard her.

'On their way,' she said, turning to the boys.

The smoke was beginning to fill the room now, and as it thickened about them, they all began to choke. They seemed to be coughing for a very long time until somewhere in the distance they could hear the welcome sound of the fire engine sirens.

The turntable ladder drew level with their window after what seemed an appallingly long time and Sam breathed a choking sigh of relief. Nan had insisted they lie on the floor where there was more air. By doing this, she had saved their lives. The rescue was all over in a matter of seconds and Sam felt a sense of unreality returning as he was lowered to the ground.

Someone threw a blanket over his shoulders as Sam stood in the street watching his home burn. Soon they would have nothing left, he thought. Maybe not even each other. Nan took him and Tim in her arms as they gazed at the flames licking the roof of the house. There was a rending, roaring, crashing sound from somewhere inside and Sam heard one of the firemen say that the first floor had collapsed. He tried to imagine what it must be like in there and thought of their home as it had been – untidy,

47

familiar, beloved. The same rage overcame him as it had when he had started to fight Alfie, and for a moment he wanted to go up to someone – anyone – and kick them hard.

Sam saw how the firemen were struggling hard to contain the fire and prevent it reaching the houses on either side. Sparks flew high in the air and the water jets lashed the burning, crumbling walls. The neighbours were evacuating their houses and great piles of possessions were being dragged out and dumped in the street. The road was very crowded now and had been sealed off by the police. There were six fire engines and a large number of police cars – all with their lights flashing – and the air seemed to reverberate with the muted clamour of radios. But subduing every other sound was the massive roaring of the flames.

'Just before you go inside, madam,' said a plain-clothes man, flashing a card that Sam could hardly see. Meanwhile, Mrs Hodgson, who had offered them a roof over their heads for the night, hovered inquisitively on her doorstep.

'Yes?' Nan's voice was oddly shrunken and Sam had never seen her look so old.

'Couple of passers-by told us they saw two men running away from the scene. They were coloured. Did you see anything yourself?'

She shook her head and pointed to Sam. 'The youngster woke us up. But I don't know if he saw anything.'

The CID man turned to Sam. 'What did you see, son?'

'There were these two blokes. They shoved something through the letter box and then they threw something else through the window. The glass broke and they ran away.' He paused and then asked curiously, 'What did they chuck in?'

'Looks like a couple of petrol bombs.'

Just then a uniformed policeman came up and took the man by the arm. He whispered something and Sam could just make out what he was saying.

'You know who this place belonged to, don't you?'

They looked at Sam and then conferred in even deeper whispers which he couldn't hear. The plain-clothes man asked Sam: 'Were the two blokes coloured, son?'

'I couldn't really see. But I don't think they were.'

'That's funny,' he replied. 'Our informants insist that they were.'

He turned briskly to Mrs Hodgson. 'Better take the kids and the old lady in now before they catch their deaths.'

We almost did, thought Sam, as he took one last glance at the burning embers of his home. What would Dad have said?

Once in Mrs Hodgson's house, they had hot drinks and then went to bed in an early dawn that smelt charred and raw. Nan did not go to bed at all but waited until the fire brigade had finished cooling down the very last smouldering ruins. Tim slept at once, but Sam could not sleep at all and at six he watched a murky dawn slowly light the road. The frost coated everything, except where the house had been. Sam had a shock when he looked out for the first time. Their house had simply vanished into a mound of smoking and steaming debris. Only one wall was still standing and the only reminder that this had been their home was a strip of the honeysuckle wallpaper that had been on the bathroom wall. A small crowd of hardy, goulish onlookers was still standing around the pyre, and the fire engines and police cars still buzzed and flashed.

At seven they had breakfast and Nan announced that she was letting Tim sleep on and that they would have the day off school. In fact they were going to have quite a few days off school for Nan added:

'We're all going down to Hastings, love. To Auntie Sue's. Just for a while.'

For a moment Sam longed to confide in her, to tell her that Mum knew something that she shouldn't and that if only she went to the police they might have no further trouble. Or things might get much worse than they already were, if possible. But Sam said nothing for he felt frozen inside. Directly they got down to Hastings he must speak to Mum himself, for however much he loved and trusted Nan she still looked like a little old lady this morning, as she lit cigarette after cigarette, making her tired eyes water.

As Mrs Hodgson fussed round them and Nan kept saying that she didn't know what they were going to do with only what they were standing up in, Sam's mind started to run at a furious rate. He kept thinking of what Wes had said in the hospital and how Uncle George was trying to blame the black people for Dad's death. And how the plain-clothes bloke had said that he had been told it was black people who had set the house alight. But Sam was sure that they hadn't been black. And then there was Alfie and Winston and all the extraordinary things that had happened before the fire. He still felt very stiff after the fight and his black eye was hurting badly.

After breakfast the police arrived to see Nan, and Sam retreated upstairs to watch Tim sleep. His mind was invaded by exhausted confusion. He wanted to go and see Wes and also to hunt down the whereabouts of Winston and his mysterious mother. But he felt too tired to do anything but sit and watch the last vestiges of smoke escape. They had all been so happy there with Dad. Now every trace of him had been removed.

The telephone rang at about nine. Mrs Hodgson bustled into the kitchen, murdering a hymn tune in a wobbling soprano. Sam was beginning to realise that Mrs Hodgson was having the time of her life.

'It's for you, Sam,' she yelled. 'He says he's a friend who's heard about the trouble.'

Sam went to the phone. Somehow he was not very surprised to recognise the rasping and whining tones of Alfie.

'You . . .' The torrent of words was obscene and violent but Sam only half took them in. Alfie concluded saying: 'So I'll get you, you little sod. You see if I don't.'

Sam held the phone away from his ear as if it were contaminated and looked around him. He was standing in the hall and could hear Mrs Hodgson back in the kitchen and see Nan slumped at the table. Gingerly, Sam put his ear back to the telephone.

'You tell your old girl what we done to you and that we'll get her too if she don't talk. Right? You got me?'

Sam put the phone down and waited for it to ring again. It did and Alfie came on with another torrent of abuse. When he had finished, he added:

'We've put the word around that the blacks did it. And you know what that means, don't yer? The first lot the Old Bill will go hunting for will be Wesley's dad and then that little sod Winston and his old girl. I'm going to fix him good for the other night and . . .'

Once again Sam put the phone down and this time it did not ring again. Desperate tiredness caught at him again, but he knew that he could no longer keep all the information to himself. He went into the dining-room and

51

looked at his poor worn-out old nan sitting at the table. Then the phone rang again and Sam rushed out into the hall. Sure enough, it was Alfie. But this time he did not have so much to say.

'You go to the Old Bill and we'll kill your mum. Now.' Then Alfie rang off and Sam began to shake all over. At last he was beginning to feel something. Sam tore into the dining-room and, with tears pouring down his face, threw his arms around Nan. He told her everything.

When Sam had finished Nan did not look so old any longer. She put her arms around him in a fierce embrace and said: 'Sam, we have some thinking to do.'

'We can't go to the police.'

'It would be best. We'll get protection that way.'

'No,' he gasped, trying to release himself from her surprisingly strong grip.

But clearly her mind was made up. She went to the phone. 'They're the only people who can help us now.'

An hour later, two plain-clothes policemen were taking a statement from Sam.

'You did the best thing, son. It's a nasty business.' They sounded reassuring but Sam didn't feel any safer.

'What about Mum?'

'We'll see she's OK. After all, she was married to a copper. And one of my best mates. We look after our own.' He stared bitterly at his companion who cleared his throat and said: 'Listen, Sam. You're a brave kid and we want you to get out of the heat for a bit. You go down to the seaside and have a little holiday with your mum. We'll look after you down there.'

'How long for?'

'Week or so. Until we've finished our investigations.'

'And nicked Uncle George and Alfie?'

'I've not heard of an Uncle George. But we got your description of Alfie.'

'You don't think it was black people who did the fire, do you?'

The plain-clothes man shrugged. 'We'll have to consider everyone till we rule them out, won't we? I mean, that's the line your dad would have taken. And he was a damn good copper.'

'Yes,' said Nan, looking up. 'He ruddy well was.'

When the police had gone and Nan was waking up Tim, Sam thought about what he had told the police and what he had left out – like Winston and his mum. Sam was determined not to do anything that would harm Dad. He loved him far too much to do that. It was like a maze. There was Dad in the centre, and spiralling out from him were the twisting avenues of Wes and his dad, Winston and his mum, Alfie and the mysterious Uncle George – and somewhere in the middle, Albino Man – who seemed so near to the heart of everything.

Part Four
The Battle of Hastings

Auntie Sue was a long-standing friend of Mum's. Her house at Hastings was called Rock View and overlooked the sea. It was part of a cluster of old Victorian buildings near the fishing boats. Because the house and the sea were so different from the grubby pavements of home, Sam felt more relaxed. But he was dazed, as they all were. Sam took refuge in the past, pushing away what had happened in Stockwell. In fact every time he thought of London, he resolutely trawled the past, coming up with so many glorious memories of Dad that he was elated. For the moment at least.

One summer visit to Hastings, Dad had taken Sam out on a chartered fishing boat and they had fished for hours on a foggy day some miles off shore. He vividly remembered the white blanketing silence and the occasional surge of the almost still water against the ribbed sides of the boat. No gulls had flown over them and it had been like living in a cotton wool world. Even the sky was so low that Sam felt he could have reached out and touched it. They hadn't caught much but they had talked to the skipper, a grizzled old man who played Radio One very loudly on his ship-to-shore radio. The thumping pop tunes had been occasionally interrupted by other skippers radioing up and talking about the weather conditions and

54

the proximity of the fish. On the way home the old fisherman had let down the nets and Sam and Dad had helped him to haul them in again. There was very little in the nets except some flat fish, some rather horrible spider crabs and a lot of pipe weed that seemed to be almost entirely made out of water.

Rock View was an enormous family seaside house in which Auntie Sue had raised a brood of children. They were grown up now and there were pictures of them all round the walls. There had never been a sign of a father and the children all looked very different. She had once owned a hotel in the town and the fatherhood of her children had always been a mystery. No one ever discussed the subject either as Auntie Sue was a rather blousy, short-tempered but extremely kind woman who did not encourage any questions about her past just as she did not expect to pry into someone else's. The house had a much lived-in feel – and Sam and Tim loved it and had often come down here with Mum and Dad to spend enjoyable fish and chippy family days and holidays.

It was memories of swimming, of Dad on holiday that cheered Sam as they took refuge from the horrors of London. Strangely, Mum was different down here and that slightly different Mum seemed to grow each day into a very different kind of Mum. Perhaps it was the absence of Dad. Perhaps it was the eagle eye and driving personality of Auntie Sue. Something was making Mum change. Sam did not know what it was but he rather liked it.

As for the fire, the police called a couple of times, interviewed Sam again and were closeted away with Mum and Nan for what seemed like hours while the boys were left to their own devices.

It was an interlude, a time when Sam instinctively knew that they were all regathering strength. But there was one thing that Sam could still not bring himself to do – tell Mum what he had promised to tell her. Every day he put if off, and every day he felt more guilty. But he still hadn't the strength. Not yet anyway.

One day, looking more positive than she had in years, Mum reached out and touched Sam's hand over the breakfast table. She seemed to have a new confidence. When she bent over him at bedtime she no longer seemed to smell of pork pie and cherries but of apricots. He wondered if she really did or was it just in his mind. It was all part of the new Mum. She suddenly seemed braver and bolder, and he sensed a new kind of determination in her.

Not only did Mum seem different herself but Sam noticed that he was beginning to feel differently towards her. He felt so much warmer and more protective. He knew now that he had to take his place as the man of the family. Sam had not thought of it like that before, but he knew that Dad would have wanted it this way.

One thing he did desperately miss was the football, and his thoughts often strayed to Wes. Sam also thought of his new-found family and wondered whether he could ever get round to discussing Winston and his mother, or even Wes, with Mum. In London it would have been unthinkable, but with her new determination anything seemed possible and he felt considerably cheered.

Then one day Auntie Sue took him aside. She had spent a good deal of time talking to Nan who, as Mum gained new drive, seemed to shrink, just as she had done immediately after the fire, with very little to say for herself or to them. It was as if her grief had suddenly consumed her and she needed time to be alone with it. Sam thought he understood this and left her alone, although Tim was just as clinging. She didn't seem to mind that, and in a way perhaps Nan needed Tim to cling to her.

Auntie Sue was a big tall woman and she dwarfed Sam as they walked together over the beach to the fishing boats. The beach smelt oily and tarry and there was a comfortable smell of fish and rope. The hump-backed fishing boats lay drawn up the beach waiting for the tide, and there were tall drying sheds, painted black, that Tim had always called Witches' Sheds. As a little boy Tim had imagined giant witches stood at the ready in the tall sheds, their giant broomsticks gripped in claw-like hands. Now Sam was reminded of this when his giant Auntie Sue overshadowed him as they walked round the sheds. They came to the smouldering embers of a fire on the beach which must have been lit by the fishermen. They sat down by it with pleasure, for although it was sunny the weather was still cold.

'Sam.'

'Mm?'

'I want to talk.'

'Yeah.'

'You sure that's OK? Because if you don't want to talk – I won't.'

'I want you to.'

'Now I've never spoken seriously to you before. After all, you had your dad and I'm not really an auntie. Just an old friend of the family.'

Sam nodded. He knew all this and wondered what she was driving at. Was she going to give him a lecture about responsibility? About replacing his dad as the head of the family. Because she needn't. He'd taken all that on board already.

'But now we should talk.'

'OK.'

For someone normally so forceful, Auntie Sue seemed oddly hesitant.

57

'You see, your dad was a bit of a lad.'

Sam sighed. 'I know all this from Nan.'

Auntie Sue nodded. 'Yes, she told me.' She paused for what seemed like a long time. 'No. This isn't another revelation. Well, at least it's about your mum. Now she's been through a lot, not that she's not brought quite a bit of it on herself. But over the last few weeks she's been under a hell of a lot of strain, and I expect you've noticed that she's beginning to stand up for herself at last. She was never an assertive woman even before you were born. She never had much confidence. But when your dad went off with that woman, well, she lost what little she had. Mark you, even in the old days, your mum couldn't show much affection. God knows, some people can't. Anyway, there were reasons on both sides and I'm not going to blame your dad for what he did. But there was something that your mum and dad did share recently. It wasn't too pleasant and he wouldn't share it with the other woman. I suppose he felt that she couldn't cope, whereas your poor old mum could. Well, whatever reasons he had, he confided in your mum, and that's why we're in the state we are – practically under police protection with your dad gone and the house burnt down and all manner of other things happening.'

'What are you on about, Auntie Sue?' asked Sam, directly he felt he could cut through the torrent of words. He had an uneasy feeling that he was going to miss something important unless he slowed her down.

'Your dad was on to someone. Someone important.'

'Uncle George?'

Auntie Sue smiled grimly. 'This man, you know, is not just another villain, black or white.'

'Who is he then?'

58

'He's someone your dad and mum knew very intimately, but now that your dad's dead no one else knows what he's been up to except your mum. And there's nothing she can do to nail him. Nothing at all. He's too well protected. And what's more, if he could shut your mum up he would.'

'Why?'

'Because he's in a position of power and he's abusing that power.'

'What kind of power?' Sam asked, desperately trying to break into this new flow of words.

'He's a copper, Sam. He's a copper. And that's why our protection is no bleeding good.' She looked into the fire with wild frightened eyes and for a moment Sam thought she was going to lose control. Meanwhile a terrifying worm of fear began to settle in his chest, winding itself so tight that he could hardly breathe.

'What can we do?' he gasped.

Auntie Sue glanced away from the fire and Sam was relieved to see that she now looked more controlled.

'How can we nail him?' asked Sam desperately. He could hardly believe in the situation. A copper behind it all? It seemed impossible. Had she gone barmy? But when Sam looked at her again he knew that she hadn't – and he also knew a new feeling was running inside him. Hatred.

'Your mum is trying to get some evidence. But if she does she's frightened the black woman's going to be dragged into it. And then your dad's name will be in the dirt. They'll say he was two-timing your mum and some of them racists will pounce on that black lady. Because she's black.'

She stood up and Sam could see that she wanted to go home. Why had she left him hanging on, like other adults had, never quite knowing what he had to do next?

Sam had a very sleepless night. Sleep seemed totally elusive. Sometimes he saw the fat cigar-smoking shape of Uncle George, and other times he saw him again but this time dressed in a policeman's uniform that seemed far too tight for him. Eventually, Sam fell into a light and dreamless sleep from which he emerged completely exhausted.

Over breakfast Mum suggested an expedition and Sam groaned aloud.

'I'm knackered, Mum.'

'Nonsense. Do you good.'

Auntie Sue looked away from him as if she was ashamed of what she had said and the way she had burdened him. Sam tried to smile at her as if to say, it doesn't matter, I wanted to learn all that. I'm old enough, after all, but he couldn't catch her eye.

'Where we going, Mum?' asked Tim helplessly.

'Somewhere or other,' she said with an abandon that Sam had never seen in her before. What on earth was happening to her? Reserved old mum would never plan anything. And here she was proposing an expedition that had no beginning, middle or end. It was so unlike her.

'Let's just go and get lost somewhere,' she said, and with a terrible lurch in his stomach, Sam suddenly realised why she was being so aimless. She really wanted them to get lost somewhere. In case they were found.

That was the first of the expeditions, attempts to find safety in a no man's land. Using little country buses they wandered through a limbo of Kent and Sussex countryside where it was possible for all three of them to melt into the obscurity of the marshes. They seemed to be three little specks in the most enormous landscape, darting and running in the safety of the great skies. The further they could see, the safer they all felt.

One late afternoon they ended up on Camber Sands, which was the greatest and flattest expanse of sand that Sam had ever seen. Mum bought them a plastic football and without quarrelling Sam and Tim played a massive one hour two-man football match. When they had finished they lay down panting beside Mum, who was sitting bolt upright behind a breakwater. This time the sun was more mellow and there was no darting wind to disturb them. The tide was miles out and the sand stretched smooth and inviting except where Sam and Tim had scuffed it up with the football.

After a while they all walked down to the water's edge, hand in hand. Sam could not remember holding his mum's hand for so long and so happily. Suddenly he felt the need to protect her, just as she felt the need to protect him. Sam suddenly realised with a guilty rush that he had not thought of Dad for a whole hour. He fixed his thoughts on his father's face but to his concern could not immediately see it. Then the face swam back into his mind with an easy glide.

They walked over muddy, sinky sand and as they did so Mum suddenly froze and panicked. It was not that sinky – only just over their ankles – and Sam could not work out whether she was afraid that it would spoil her shoes or she was really afraid of sinking further down in it. She began to cry in a flurry of frustration and helplessness and Sam's protective instincts became even stronger. She looked round her desperately and Sam tried to take over and reassure her.

'Lean on me, Mum.'

But he had not reckoned with Tim's enthusiasm.

'No,' he said. 'Lean on me, Mum. I'm stronger than him anytime.'

The results were predictably disastrous. Not knowing whom to satisfy or whom to lean on, she leant on both at once and neither were ready for her. As a result they all fell down into the mud in an undignified heap. For a moment Sam did not know whether she was going to laugh or cry. For a moment she was clearly not sure herself, and then she began to laugh.

'I've ruined my coat!' she shrieked.

'I love you, Mum.'

Staggering to her feet, she made ineffective attempts to wipe herself down.

Sam laughed again. 'Don't worry, Mum. It'll brush off,' he said.

Then they quietened, for they both realised that Tim was ignoring them and staring very hard at the distant beach.

'Someone's watching us,' he said in a wooden voice, but when they turned round all they could see was a tiny figure hurrying off in the direction of a closed café.

'Just a man taking his dog for a walk,' Mum said.

'But there's no dog,' said Tim.

Suddenly their attention was very quickly distracted.

'The water,' said Sam. 'Look. It's cutting us off.'

And it was. Long green swathes of water were covering the sand to their right at a very alarming rate, and there was no doubt that they might have to wade back. Worse was to follow; on one side there was a long deep-looking channel that barred their way, and when Sam looked on the other side he could see that the shallow water was rushing fast into a kind of trench. They were rapidly being isolated on a sandy plateau and they had the choice of two evils to contend with. Either shallow water and a sudden drop, or deeper water that looked as if it might become deeper still.

There was no time to be lost. Sam suddenly remembered that Mum couldn't swim.

'Come on, Mum,' Sam yelled. 'Tim!' He began to drag them towards the channel and as he did so felt a rush of exhilaration; he was in charge. He wished suddenly that one of the girls at school could have been watching. They began to wade through the water that was so cold their feet immediately went numb.

'We'd better run,' said Sam, lugging at Mum, who was gasping and laughing and floundering all at the same time. She was small and dumpy and Sam had the impression that she was beginning to look like a stumpy galleon under sail. Very erratic sail. The water deepened in the centre of the channel and began to inch its way above Mum's knees. She screamed. Meanwhile the water was round Tim's waist and well up Sam's thighs. Then, just as the boys thought they might have to swim for it, the water became shallower, until they were running up the smooth sand with the water back round their ankles. But it was so cold the returning flow of blood was hideously painful. Tim began to cry, but to everyone's surprise Mum said:

'Don't be a baby, Tim. We must run to keep warm. Come on!' and she began to run quite fast.

Sam stared after her in amazement. He felt again the onrush of love that he had experienced before. But this time even more strongly.

Gradually their feet thawed out and by luck they found a small transport café near the bus stop, where they drank mugs of strong tea sweetened with condensed milk and ate great wads of bacon sandwiches. It was luxury of a kind none of them had enjoyed before. On the bus back

63

they felt like singing, and were only put off doing so by the other grim-faced passengers.

But the idyll was not to last. The next day they took a bus to Dungeness. Tim wanted to go on the railway and Sam was curious to see the nuclear power station. They had never been there before but he could remember Dad talking about it as one of the best fishing spots in the south. He could hear his voice saying: 'It's on a curve of the coast with a deeply shelving beach.'

When they arrived Sam thought it was the bleakest place he had ever seen. The pebbles stretched for miles and the power station crouched by the sea like some great wounded animal. Little shanties and clapboard bungalows littered the pebble beach; in fact it was not really a beach at all, but just a great pebble-strewn wasteland. Wild sea cabbage and various other straggly-looking plants grew amongst the pebbles and there was a smell of seaweed and desolation mixed with tar and pitch and rotting wood. But they could see the railway line and the lighthouse and they began to walk towards them with anticipation. Once again they could see for miles and the huge expanse made them feel safe. It was a damp Tuesday morning and there seemed hardly anyone around. The sea made a shifting grinding sound on the farthermost pebbles and there was a thin gauze of rain in the air. They walked stolidly on without talking, content in their own company, feeling safe. They didn't see the line of motorcycles until they were almost at the lighthouse. The bikers were hidden behind a low sea wall.

'We got company,' said Mum in an uninterested voice, and only Tim, who was interested in motorbikes, continued to stare at them. Then, as they walked on, the bikes started to rev up. Slowly they began to drive towards them in a neat formation that seemed to stay miraculously intact despite the pebbles and hollows and ruts and bumps that they were travelling over. The line came on, and they stopped to stare. Tim and Mum and Sam. Mum in the centre. Hand in hand. Defenceless. Then Sam recognised the middle rider of the six. It was Alfie.

Alfie was thin, gaunt, stick-like and menacing. He was also grinning like a starved wolf.

Sam looked at the lighthouse. It was only yards away now. Just yards.

'Run!' he screamed.

But neither Mum nor Tim moved an inch.

'What?' asked Tim weakly.

'I said run, you thick idiot,' yelled Sam. Somehow Mum got the message and dragged at Tim's hand.

'Come on, love. Do what Sam says.'

'Bloody run!' said Sam. And they were running now, far faster than they had run against the tide. Far faster than they had ever run before. Over the skidding pebbles to the lighthouse while the bikes roared behind them. They made the lighthouse within inches of the scorching tyres and panted at the entrance, staring almost insanely at the old man who confronted them.

'Want to come up?' he asked expressionlessly, seeming not to see the six motorbikes revving just behind the garden wall that had saved them from the gang.

'Course we're coming up,' said Mum. 'We got nowhere else to go.'

For a moment Sam had been afraid that Alfie and his bikers would follow them up the long staircase inside the lighthouse, but he heard them rev up and drive away. Half-way up the stairs, Sam paused panting and drew Tim and Mum towards him. They huddled together protectively in the confined space. Even through the solid walls of the lighthouse Sam was sure that he could hear the roar of bikes.

'That was the bloke who beat me up, or tried to. He's mixed up in it all.'

Sam had expected Mum to hedge or to fluster or to deny all the things that he knew and Nan knew and even Auntie Sue knew. But he was wrong. Quite wrong. Mum was completely in control.

'I might have expected they'd pick us up and follow us.' She took a long cool glance at the terrified and completely bewildered Tim and said to Sam: 'I'll talk to you about all this when we get home.' She spoke to Sam as if he were her equal. He tried to think rationally but all he could think about was a triumphant Alfie exacting his revenge by beating him to a pulp with the support of all his friends. It could so easily happen and who could prevent it? Then he looked at Mum and he felt a child again. She would solve everything, wouldn't she?

In fact she did. 'Right.' She gripped her handbag fiercely in one hand and tied her scarf more firmly around her head. Then she glanced down at Tim who was looking very frightened. 'You stay close to me,' she snapped. 'And you, Sam. Stay behind me.'

'Yes, Mum,' they chorused, and dutifully did as they were bid.

Mum began to descend the lighthouse stairs. Her lips were compressed and her step was firm and Sam was reminded of Queen Boadicea in a bad mood. He could well imagine Mum climbing into a chariot with spikes on the wheels and riding hell for leather at Alfie and his companions.

As it was, she ground to a halt by the old man at the entrance. Super Mum, thought Sam, and suddenly he

66

could see her sprouting wings. From an unassuming housewife into Wonder Woman. She spoke firmly to the old man.

'We've got a problem.'

'Somethin' wrong with the stairs?' He looked vaguely up the well of the lighthouse.

'No,' said Mum firmly. 'The problem's outside.'

He looked perplexed and Mum continued briskly: 'There are some motorbike yobs outside who are molesting us. I want you to call the police.'

The police? wondered Sam. Were they perhaps the last people they should call in the circumstances? Then he told himself that he was being an idiot. The local police couldn't possibly be caught up in Dad's business.

The old man stared at Mum and then his head began to nod as if he had the palsy.

'Yobboes?' He looked out of the door and just on cue they roared past. He waved his fist at them and snarled: 'I'll get the coppers all right. We had a lot of trouble last year and . . . ' He dissolved into muttering and then sprang to the phone. He began to dial. 'You stay with me, lady,' he said. 'Wait till them coppers come.'

'Right,' said Mum. 'We'll take your advice.'

They didn't have to wait long. Two police Range Rovers appeared on the horizon in a few minutes, and directly they saw them coming, Alfie's bikers tried to beat a hasty retreat. They roared across the hard-packed pebbles, sending up little spumes of dusty weed and sea cabbage. But there was nowhere they could go unless they turned round and plunged into the sea. All they could do was to sweep in wide arcs away from the police cars who had now split up and were converging on them.

After five minutes of desultory circling, the cars caught up with the bikes and the hopeless chase was at an end.

The policemen got out of their Range Rovers and the boys got off their bikes and there was a flurried conference. Then one of the policemen drove over to them while the others remained guarding the bikers.

Meanwhile the old man had worked himself up into a fine pitch of excitement and was wailing and ranting in the doorway. 'That'll learn 'em,' he kept saying over and over again, with irritating monotony. But Sam was hardly paying attention to anything; he just couldn't get over the change in Mum. From a woman who never knew her own mind, she now acted as if she really did. Had it taken Dad's death to change her, or was there another reason?

The policeman got out of his car by the lighthouse and smiled at them. He was rather chubby and had a bobbing movement to his whole body as if he was bowing cheerily in front of them.

'You been having trouble then?'

Immediately Mum spoke out. 'We certainly have. Directly we arrived these awful boys started circling round us. My kids were terrified.'

Sam felt ashamed. Hadn't he fought Alfie and won? At least with Winston's help.

The policeman was bobbing at them again. 'Don't you worry. There's obviously a lot wrong with their bikes and we're going to take them in. Do you want to press any charges?'

Mum shook her head. 'Just as long as they go away.'

'What was wrong with their bikes, mister?'

Both Mum and Sam turned on Tim in an attempt to shut him up, but the policeman seemed pleased to answer him.

'You interested in bikes, son?'

'You bet.'

'Gonna have a bike of your own a bit later?'

'If they'll let me,' he said balefully, not looking at Mum and Sam but somehow meaning them.

'Then you keep it in better nick than them lot. All kinds of things wrong, I bet. Brakes. Lights. All kinds of things.'

Tim nodded, for once in awe of someone. 'My dad was a copper,' he blurted out. 'But he's dead now.'

There was a short and uncomfortable silence during which Mum, Sam and the policeman tried to find something to say. Then the policeman stretched out his hand and slowly ruffled Tim's fair hair.

'I'm sorry, son.' He looked at Mum and then at Sam. He had stopped bobbing.

Once the police had taken the bikers away Mum suddenly lost all her authority, and Sam realised how much it had taken out of her.

'You were great, Mum,' said Sam.

She looked at him, slightly flushed, and Sam could see that one of her hands was trembling very noticeably.

'Like a cup of tea?' asked the old man. They all nodded enthusiastically and he went away and came back not only with tea but chocolate biscuits too. The boys ate them hungrily, but Mum sat quietly sipping her tea. Her hand was still shaking and the cup rattled in its saucer. The old man watched her for a bit, but he was tactful enough not to say anything or even to respond to the knowledge that their dad was dead. Sam could have killed Tim for blurting it out like that, but he had felt oddly touched when the policeman had ruffled Tim's hair. Then a cloud fell across the image in his mind, and he saw again the bulky shape of Uncle George.

When they had finished their tea, they said goodbye to the old man and he watched them go with a kind protectiveness that made Sam want to cry. He felt very sad now, and for the first time in days, sharp images of Dad kept appearing in his mind. As they walked down to the sea, Sam could see Dad running in front of them and then doing one of his silly walks – a kind of weird high-stepping that the boys had loved to watch. This was what he had wanted – Dad's presence to come alive again. But ironically he no longer wanted that now. All Sam could feel was a stabbing pain that choked him up inside.

They eventually found the sea at the bottom of a steeply shelving beach. To Sam it was the cruellest sea he had ever seen, and even Tim seemed upset by it. It was very deep and dark green and kind of angrily boiling. As Dad had said, this seemed to be the very edge of the coastline, and a few hundred yards out was an iron gantry with a bell on it. Every so often the bell tolled miserably, and Sam supposed it was warning ships off the outfall of the power station which crouched behind them, looking like something out of a science fiction film. It was the most hostile place he had ever seen, and it exactly suited his mood.

The three of them sat hunched on the pebbles, watching the boiling sea. Now the images of Dad had been replaced by those of Uncle George. Sam could see him now in his policeman's uniform, smoking his Havana cigar. He was standing by the sea and then he began to walk into it, or rather on it. Blimey, thought Sam, he can walk on the water. Uncle George turned round and leered at them.

Mum seemed to have lost all her bounce as she sat there shivering. Their escape was over and she knew it. Sam knew it too and Tim, affected by their mood, stared dolefully out to sea without even throwing any stones in it. For a ridiculous moment Sam wondered if he could see Uncle George too, but he knew he couldn't.

Sam felt wretched. They had been found out in their hidey hole and once more his family was under attack. Beside him, Mum buried her head in her coat as if it was all to much to bear. Suddenly Sam saw his dad again, throwing stones across the sea at Uncle George. Then Dad turned and said something in Sam's mind. You're the man of the house now, he said, and disappeared. But Uncle George remained where he was, leering at them again. How Sam hated him and how he wished he could beat him to a pulp.

Sam stood up and sat down again, pushing himself in between Mum and Tim. Then he put his arms around them and they sat together, watching the sea spitting angrily on the pebbles. It was so deep; there could be no question of even paddling. Sam had the idea that the sea would seize their ankles if they did and rush them out, beyond Uncle George and out and down into some dark and sinuous underwater kingdom from which they would never return. A kingdom ruled by Uncle George and Alfie and Albino Man. A kingdom of livid and pale colour, hung with fronds of seaweed that smelt of cigar smoke and motorbike oil and old cinema seats.

'All those horrid things aren't going to start happening again, are they?' whined Tim.

'Not if I'm around,' said Sam grandly.

Their journey back to Hastings was doleful and uneventful. Tim was exhausted when they got back to the house and Nan, looking a little less subdued, took him up to bed, grumbling affectionately in her old way. Auntie Sue was out and Mum and Sam went up to the Wimpy Bar for a talk. It was a quiet evening up there and only a few tables were occupied. Sam had a hamburger and a milk shake while Mum had a cup of tea that she said was awful.

'I'm going to come straight to the point with you, Sam. You're just on fourteen and you're old enough to know some things I would never have told you a couple of years ago. And I'm really only telling you now because your dad's dead.' She paused and took a draught of brackish tea. 'Over the last year your dad found out something that probably caused his death. You've got to realise that your dad was a very brave man.'

Sam nodded his head impatiently. He knew that.

'There's nothing worse than a bent copper.' She paused again and then rushed on. 'It brings everything down. Anyway, your dad was keeping a watch for drugs on one of the estates and he found an awful lot were being used. He knew who was getting it. He found out that they were being sheltered by one of his bosses. By someone who should have known better than putting his job on the line by doing a cover up.'

'Which boss?'

'We don't know.'

But Sam wasn't having any of that. 'You do, Mum,' he said firmly. 'That's why it's all been happening. Alfie, and the house being burnt out.'

She shook her head.

'Why can't you just tell and it'll all be over?'

She shook her head again. 'It's not as easy as that, Sam. I don't know. And that's God's honest truth. But I do know who does.'

'Who?'

'Albino Man,' she said quietly.

Sam just stared at her, unable to believe in what she was saying.

'What?'

'I know you lot are scared of him. But he's a good man. He's been one of your dad's contacts for years.'

'A grass?'

'Maybe. But not a grass who did it for money. He did it for the good of the community.' She looked at Sam, knowing that he didn't believe her. But in fact he did not know what to think.

'So why does he know about the bent copper?'

'He knows all the villains. Black and white. And it was he who tipped your dad off in the first place. And your dad checked and double-checked. And found out that Albino Man was right. Dead right.'

'But how did *you* know all this?' asked Sam almost accusingly, and Mum winced. Immediately Sam wished he had not spoken, but she ignored him, carrying on with her own train of thought.

'You know your dad didn't – I didn't – we didn't get on that well. You know he had someone else. Someone who was black.'

Sam nodded, and then told her the part he had held back. He told her about Winston and how he had helped him in his fight with Alfie and how he had discovered that Winston was his half-brother. Mum almost seemed relieved when he told her and tears flooded down her cheeks.

'She's not a bad woman. She's a good woman. And it was my fault I let him go. And some of those coppers are so prejudiced. If they'd found him going with a black woman, it would have been the end of him in the police. They'd have made life unbearable for him at the nick.' She continued to weep and Sam hoped that no one was watching.

'But Dad confided in you then,' he said, hoping she would stop crying.

'Yes.'

'When?'

'We'd always had a deepness between us. Even if he couldn't feel my love he could feel my support. Perhaps more than hers. Or maybe he felt he didn't want to get her into danger, and I could take it or something. I'll never know. But I'm glad he told me. Glad.'

'What did he tell you?' Sam's voice shook. Now he was afraid. He looked furtively round the Wimpy Bar, to see if there were strangers there.

'It happened a few months ago. He'd just come back from football training and you two were in bed. I shall never forget that evening.' As his mother talked, Sam lost all interest in his present surroundings and saw them again, sitting in that room. Dad was gone, the room was gone, but Sam was back there in that passage of time, and Mum held him entranced in a past that he would never want to leave.

'It was an early summer evening and I remember a couple of cats were fighting in the garden and your dad went out to shoo them away. Well, when he came in he sat back in that chair of his and he said, "Mary, girl, I've got something to tell you that you must remember if anything happens to me." I kidded him a bit, saying nothing would ever happen, but he was serious and do you know, I think it was the first time I've ever seen your dad real scared. Well, he said that he'd been looking out for some right villains and that he'd found out a copper was mixed up in it. Taking money from them and protecting them. I could hardly believe my ears, but he was dead serious, I can tell you. Naturally, I asked who this bent copper was, but he wouldn't tell me, said the only person who knew besides him was the grass. Albino Man. And he was sure that he was right. In fact Albino Man had got the proof, but he didn't say what the proof was. But then he said that if anything did happen to him I wasn't to contact Albino Man. It was too dangerous and he made me swear that I wouldn't. Instead, Albino Man was to contact me. And he might not do it right away. I might have to wait.'

'But why doesn't Albino Man go straight to the police?'

'Because he wanted me to take the name to Bill Frost. You know, Dad's old mate in the CID. It would all need firming up, he said, and Bill could do it. And if Albino Man just went to any copper it wouldn't work.'

'So why doesn't he go to Bill? Why do you have to be dragged into it?'

'Albino Man would never go to Bill. He hates him. He got him nicked years ago for something he says he didn't do, so he wouldn't do him any favours. No way. At least that's what your dad said.'

'But after all these things that've happened,' said Sam. 'To all of us. Why didn't you go to Albino Man? If you had, maybe the house . . .'

She held up her hand wearily. 'Don't think I haven't wanted to. But I promised your dad. I promised him.' She began to cry again. 'It was the only time in years he ever asked me to do anything for him and he was dead serious. If I break that promise I feel I've lost him for ever. Do you understand, Sam?'

'Yes, Mum,' said Sam. 'I do understand. Now what?' he asked after a long silence.

She looked at him in surprise, as if he had asked a very stupid question. 'We must wait, wait till Albino Man comes. Your dad said.' She looked at him wide-eyed and he knew it was hopeless. She had to hang on to that special bond. In a way she was crazy, for the more she hung on the more danger they were in. And in a peculiar kind of way she knew that. But he understood why that bond was more important than anything. Than anyone. Than them. It was a shocking fact but there it was. It was as if Mum had been suspended in time by a dead man. Yet incredibly strengthened, too. His death had brought them back to each other and because of it they could all die.

Sam watched her finish her tea. He knew what he had to do.

Part Five
Albino Man

That night Sam could not sleep again but he felt better. Dad's death was doing something for them all. Mum had got a better grip, but not enough by any means to save their lives. He had to do that, and be mature enough to undertake the most dangerous journey of his life. But what had Dad's death done for Tim? Sam felt a sudden rush of affection for his little brother. Actually it hadn't done anything for him. Not yet. He was too dazed and too much of a baby – their baby now. Sam suddenly felt what it was like to be a parent. It was weird, as if he and Mum were married and Tim was their child. Then he thought of Nan. Slowly she was regaining her old strength and was showing it by nagging away at Tim. Sam grinned in the darkness. Poor old Tim – he was always coming in with mud on his shoes or a dirty face or with his trainers all scuffed up. Nan pounced on him every time and Tim moaned and groaned. But it was doing Nan a power of good – and it was great to see her returning to her bossy old self.

Sam had already raided Tim's money box and Mum's purse. He had never done this before, and he was praying that she would not check her bag tonight. If she did he was done. Completely done.

Nothing had happened so far and he had heard her go to bed. Auntie Sue had been the last to come in and he suspected that she had had a few as she stumbled up the stairs and went slowly and snortingly to bed. His plan was to rise at five and catch the early train to London. The very earliest there was. Then he would go straight to Albino Man and find out the name of the bent copper. After that he would go down the nick and find Dad's mate and give him the name and then it would all be over and they would be left in peace. He thought of Alfie. Well – maybe if the bent copper was nicked they'd get Alfie too. They seemed connected in some way, although he did not understand what way. When it was all cleared up he would ring Mum and tell her and he would find the way to Winston and his mother. They'd be able to tell him all kinds of things he didn't know about Dad, and he would be able to relive new parts of his life. And in return – well, he would have plenty of memories to share too, wouldn't he?

Sam counted the money again. He had about forty quid – not bad and surely more than enough. Still you had to think of the unexpected, and all this could be very unexpected. But Sam did not feel afraid. He did not even think of being afraid. It was amazing for he had always been terrified of Albino Man. But now he just saw him as a means to an end. There was only one problem. He didn't know Winston's address, and the only person who could tell him was Nan. If he asked her, she would surely stop him. Then, in his new-found mood of optimism, Sam thought of a solution. When he had sorted everything out he would call Nan and she would be so pleased that she would give him the address. It was neat, too neat, and he knew it. But he chose to ignore it. Like one or two other things.

Sam tucked the alarm clock under the bedclothes and prayed that no one would hear it when it went off. Luckily the house was big enough for him to have his own room or he would have been well and truly blown. Just as he was about to drop off to sleep, Sam wondered if he would have time to visit Wes.

The alarm clock woke him spot on time, but fortunately woke no one else. It was a very good start, but directly he got up, Sam found the false confidence of last night had evaporated and he was afraid, terribly afraid. He stood there, shivering in the early dawn. The whole schedule, the whole idea now seemed completely insane. The more he thought about it the more idiotic it became. Still trembling, Sam got a grip on himself. If Mum could cope, surely he could.

Sam silently let himself out of the house and walked from the old town towards the station. He wore a parka, sweater and jeans. There had been a very sharp frost overnight and it had made the pavements slippery. A few early workers drove past him and somewhere a milk cart clinked and rattled. He hoped he would not run into a copper or some busybody adult; he didn't, and although the station was a long way he eventually made it. But the fear never left him, holding Sam in a frozen embrace that was as hard as the frost that covered the seats on the esplanade with a cold rime.

The first train left at five thirty, and Sam sat hunched in a corner seat watching the landscape slip past. Soon they were out in the country and the frost was even more apparent. Trees and bushes were clad in a kind of glittering mantle that looked as vicious as the sea at Dungeness.

It seemed ages before the train arrived in London, and Sam felt trapped in a cocoon of terror. By the time they reached Charing Cross he was shivering as hard as he had been when he first awoke. He made himself leave the

79

train, although it had crossed his mind that he might just stay on it until it travelled back to Hastings. But something drove him on.

Sam had left a note outside his mum's door. It read quite simply: DON'T WORRY. I'VE GONE TO SORT THINGS OUT. WILL RING AT LUNCHTIME. He had Auntie Sue's number in his pocket.

He caught the tube to Stockwell, and now that he was on such familiar territory his fear lessened a little and he stopped shivering, although the butterflies in his stomach that replaced it were just as bad. But the familiarity of his surroundings began to be more and more reassuring and Sam recovered some of his determination.

It was after half past seven when Sam arrived at Stockwell and the commuter battle had already begun. Street cleaners were out and a café smelled wonderfully of hot toast. Although he had not eaten anything, Sam did not want to stop anywhere. He went into a sweet shop and bought a couple of Mars Bars. Feeling much better, he munched them as he walked towards the cinema. It suddenly occurred to him that he might be far too early for Albino Man, and the thought of more waiting made him panic. The fear began to drum at him again. He had no idea of where Albino Man lived, and the thought of searching for him or, worse still, hanging around until there was a sign of life at the cinema filled him with horror. But in fact he was lucky, for as he came alongside the dark hulk of the frost-glittering building he could see that the front doors were open. Lucky? Sam wondered as he walked slowly towards the dilapidated and cavernous entrance.

The interior of the cinema foyer smelt of Jeyes Fluid. There was also another smell that was indefinable for a while and then Sam suddenly realised it was cats. The plasterwork had been gaudily painted over in rapidly fading murals of rock stars and surreal scenes reminiscent of pop videos. In the centre of what had once been an elegant thirties' foyer was a box office that also served as a confectionery stall. There were a large number of peeling posters of rock groups and one or two fading photographs stuck untidily on the front of an empty glass cabinet.

In the early morning the entire foyer radiated a terrible gloom, and as there was no sign of life Sam overcame his fear and entered the auditorium for the first time in his life.

The sheer size of the desolate auditorium amazed him. Here the smell of cats and cinema seats was more intense. Sam looked up at the darkened ceiling and saw a run-down Moorish palace. There were balconies and boxes and alcoves and murals and thin half moons, all covered in Moorish design and script. It was difficult to make out some of the murals because they were so dark and dirty and dingy, but he could vaguely see a palace and a lake and some tall people with turbans feeding some animals. Were they tame tigers?

Suddenly Sam felt so tired that he was afraid he would faint; he sat down quickly on one of the ripped-up disgusting-looking cinema seats. There was still no sign of life and he was so tired. He must have dozed for a moment; there was a swishing sound and when he looked up he saw to his amazement that the curtains in front of the stage were gradually opening and a rather grey-looking cinema screen was gradually being lowered until it was almost level with the floor.

There was a furred blast of music, and Sam sat bolt upright, the hairs tingling and slowly rising on the back of his neck and for a few seconds he was so surprised by this that he forgot to be afraid. Instead he gazed in amazement at the almost demonic fairytale scene that was opening up in front of his eyes. A beautiful Indian princess stood up and began to walk down castle steps similar to the faint murals on the walls. She burst into song and the dusty, dreary auditorium was filled with clear cut and jangly eastern music. Then, after a few seconds, the film and the soundtrack suddenly wailed to a slow motion halt.

Standing up, Sam wanted to run, and yet his feet felt as if they were lead. For a moment the heaviness remained and he couldn't move. Then his strength miraculously returned and he started to run towards the exit. The doors by the entrance to the foyer seemed to have closed and yet Sam ran on, his breath coming in little grunts and gasps, the tears of blind panic forming in his eyes. As the darkness closed in on him an even darker shape reared up in front of him. Cold hands pressed round his face and Sam struggled, screaming out in shock. He found himself propelled by the shoulders into the foyer and then saw that he was looking up at Albino Man.

'Isn't my cinema beautiful?' he said in his light, sing-song voice. 'At least it can be very beautiful when the lights go out. I was just running through one of my lovely Asian films. That's all we show nowadays – the occasional Indian film and all those noisy people jumping up and down on the stage and making the ugly sounds that . . .' His excited high voice petered away but he still kept his long sinewy arms around Sam's shoulders. 'I know who you are,' he said and bent down towards him.

They walked through the foyer to a poky little office full of cats. They seemed to sit on every surface and they all gave Sam a rather hostile look as he came in. But he was no longer afraid; after all he was in the lion's den now and there was no going back.

'Don't worry about the cats,' said Albino Man. 'They're my family. Now would you like a bacon sandwich?'

Sam suddenly realised that he was ravenously hungry; the two Mars Bars seemed ages away. 'Yes, please.'

'Have mine. I was just going to have breakfast.'

Sam greedily took it and as he brought it to his lips the most beautiful aroma came up to him. He bit into the sandwich; it was delicious, with bread soft yet crusty and the bacon crisp and succulent. It was the best bacon sandwich he had ever tasted.

Sam had four bacon sandwiches in the end and two cups of very strong tea with lots of sugar. Albino Man kept going out into a little kitchen next door and making him sandwiches and Sam had completely forgotten his fear and the reason he had come to see him. He was living for the moment in an oasis of warmth and well-being. Then just as he was contemplating a fifth bacon sandwich he suddenly came to and remembered everything.

Sam sat bolt upright and stared up into the pink irises of Albino Man, but before he spoke he was interrupted.

'You remember the time I chased after you and you ran away over the common. Just after your dad died.'

'Yes.'

'I was trying to tell you then,' Albino Man said.

'Trying to tell me?'

'You know the score.'

'Eh?'

Albino Man looked at him impatiently. 'Come on, son. About your dad.'

'You mean –'

'I mean I know why you've come and I tried to tell you before, but I'm a frightened man now. Yes, a very frightened man.' Sam looked up and believed him.

'Otherwise I would have found you.'

'Yeah.'

'But now you found me. Right?'

'Right.'

'You see, son, I know who the guy is and I have papers in that safe that would put him away for years.'

'What papers?' Sam was suddenly astute.

'Transcripts of some tapes your dad took when he was doing a surveillance. And I've got the tapes put away at the back of the stage. But I need the money, man. Lots of money to get me out of here and back to Jamaica. I don't want to leave my lovely picture palace, but they're gonna pull it down soon anyway and that's a crying shame but someone's gonna pull me down pretty fast and that'll be it. I'll be a stiff. See?'

'Yeah.'

'Sonny, I want you to go and fetch that policeman and bring him down here. And when he sees these papers he'll pay. Good and strong.'

'Can't you go to him?'

'I daren't leave this place, sonny. Here I can duck and weave and hide and I've got my hidey hole. But once I leave this place they'll find me. They're watching for me all the time.'

Sam didn't know whether to believe him or not. 'If they're watching they'd have seen me.' Who are they? Sam wondered desperately.

'They won't start this early,' began Albino Man.

'Won't they?' asked an all-too-familiar voice, and Sam turned to see Alfie standing by the door of the office. For a moment he wondered why the cats hadn't moved. Then he saw that they had frozen in their chairs and on the tables. 'Hi!' said Alfie, moving towards Sam. 'I have a couple of scores to settle with you.'

Sam edged round the small office table, looking into Alfie's mean little eyes with all the terror of a rabbit hypnotised by a snake. At the same time he felt oddly calm and collected, and there was a steely feeling in him that was quite different from when he had lost his temper on the recreation ground. Quietly Alfie moved towards him, his lips curling in a sardonic grin.

'Stay where you are.' The light voice was charged with threat and Alfie stopped in his tracks. His hands went to his greasy jeans and he struggled to pull something out of his sock. But Albino Man was too fast for him. He kicked Alfie round the back of the knees and he collapsed on the ground with a funny little gasp. Then Albino Man bent over and did something else to Alfie. Sam was never sure what it was, but the next time he looked at him Alfie was again measuring his length on the ground. The recreation ground, the floor of the supermarket and now here at the cinema. Sam was getting used to Alfie lying prone.

'He'll live,' said Albino Man in reply to Sam's questioning gaze. 'But the others are outside and if he doesn't show –' He went to the safe and pulled out some papers, putting them in a grubby envelope. Sam rammed it into one of his parka pockets. 'Go out the back way. I'll show you.' Albino Man hurried out through the foyer and back into the darkened auditorium. He moved with tremendous silent speed and Sam ran to catch up with him. As they dashed through the cinema towards the screen and stage, Sam again saw the faded tigers on the wall. Of course. Albino Man reminded him of a tiger, with his lithe stealth and sudden springing movements.

'Will you be OK?' asked Sam as they paused on the stage.

Albino Man grinned. 'You bet. I have my hidey hole and that's where the tapes are and I'm going there until your dad's mate shows up.' He went to the back of the stage and pressed a button on the wall. Almost silently a small section of the floor slid open to reveal a dark hole and an iron ladder leading downwards. Albino Man picked up a fire extinguisher that was lying on the stage and put it on a bracket that exactly covered the button. 'Not bad, eh? And what's more I can lock the trap door from underneath and make myself snug. I've got a couple of thermos flasks down there.'

'What about the cats?'

'I always take them with me.'

Sam tried to picture Albino Man and his cats in the stuffy little hole. He failed to do this but somehow he could smell them. Albino Man climbed into his lair and Sam stared around him. How was he going to get out? And wouldn't Alfie be coming to?

'You go down towards the right and there's a door that leads on to the street. You'll be safe there.' He called his cats and they scampered towards him. Then he drew the hatch down and he and they disappeared.

'I'll be back soon,' whispered Sam to no one. How strange, thought Sam, he's not a nightmare any longer. He's a friend – a kind of friend – of Dad's.

The door opened on to the busy high street and there was no sign of the bikers. Sam hurried to the underground station, the big envelope in his parka pocket feeling red hot and obtrusive. The nick was in Brixton High Road and it would be quicker to take the tube. Once he had dived underground and bought his ticket, Sam began to feel more uneasy. He glanced at his watch; it was ten o'clock. The morning rush hour was finished and the tube tunnels had a nasty deserted look. But nothing happened as he rode the escalator and looked at posters for faraway places and ladies' underwear.

The platform was almost deserted as he waited for the train and he kept looking at the entrances and exits, praying that they would remain empty. He seemed to be waiting for ever. Still the platform remained deserted; still the train did not come. Gradually the waiting became unbearable and all his former fears returned. He began to sweat. Still nothing happened and still no train came.

Then Sam saw them slouch on to the platform. There was no sign of Alfie but the others were all there, and they had seen him. With a great cheer they ran towards him, five white skinheads with dirty leather jackets, Doc Martens even bigger than Alfie's and Union Jack T-shirts. They ran towards him with a howl of delight, and Sam could only stare hopelessly at the black entrance to the tunnel.

He was saved by a group of schoolchildren who suddenly burst on to the platform with their teacher. The bikers stopped in their tracks, knowing that they could do nothing for the moment. Sam almost laughed in triumph as he saw the frustration in their faces and their looks of outrage and fury. The scent of the chase was on and Sam knew he was the quarry; he was determined to outwit the gang and reach the nick in safety. After all, he only had to travel one station, and if he got in with the school kids he would be safe. The train eventually rumbled in, and just as the doors shut he saw Alfie stumble on to the platform. The gang were already on board, and although he tried to wrench the doors open, the train was moving out of the station. It was too late. Sam permitted himself a gentle wave as Alfie's rage-contorted features slid past the window. The hunt was on and Sam had won the first round. But he could not have done so without the help of the haunter of his nightmares: Albino Man.

The train rattled into Brixton and hissed to a halt. Sam was through the doors in an instant, but so were the gang. Once again luck was on Sam's side for the entrance was ahead of him and they were delayed by an old lady laden with bags who was walking slowly in front of them. They would have barged over her, but the bikers were too cautious to spoil the hunt and draw too much attention to themselves at this stage of the game. Sam knew they would either try to get him in the tunnel or on the escalators, particularly if not many people were around. But Sam had a ruse. An off-duty black London Transport guard was walking in front of him and Sam quickly caught up with him.

'Mister.'

He swung round.

'Them boys are chasing me. Will you help me?'

'That lot?'

'Yeah.'

'You come with me then.'

They walked silently up the tunnel together, turning round now and then to see the bikers marching steadily behind them.

'What you done to them?'

'Nothing. I'm taking something to the nick. Something they want.'

'I get it, or at least I don't. But you need protection, man.'

'Yeah.'

'You got it.'

'Thanks.'

'Can you run?'

'Reckon.'

'In a minute we're gonna break into a gallop.'

'Right.'

'And we're gonna gallop right on down to the nick.'

'You bet.'

They walked on tensely for another few yards and then he said:

'Leg it.'

And they did.

Directly Sam and the guard began to run, so did the bikers. And they could run.

'Come on, man,' yelled the guard and they literally flew up towards the escalator. But the gang were gaining and as they reached the escalator they were only a few feet behind them. Some followed them directly up while others jumped on the slippery sides and ran acrobatically along them, but Sam and the guard still had the edge on them, despite the fact that Sam was sure he could feel their hot breath on the back of his neck.

Somehow they reached the top, gasping and panting, and there in front of them was the ticket barrier. Suddenly with horror Sam realised he had not got his ticket. He didn't dare pause to search in his trouser pocket.

'No ticket,' he gasped.

'No problem,' panted the young guard.

They flashed through the barrier, past the ticket collector who looked as if he weighed in at about nineteen stone.

'Trouble,' yelled the guard as they rushed past him. 'Get that lot.'

'Right on.' The giant beamed with pleasure and stepped out into the path of the oncoming bikers. 'Now I want to check the tickets of you boys,' he said in a threatening voice.

Over his shoulder, Sam saw the gang pause, wondering if they might chance their luck. Then he saw them stop and begin to check their pockets.

He was safe.

Alfie stood in front of the station entrance, his bike parked illegally on a yellow line.

''Nother one,' said Sam to his protector.

The guard walked up to Alfie and said quietly: 'I'm taking this kid up the nick. You cause any trouble and there are two coppers over there that I'll shop you to.'

'Trouble?' asked Alfie sweetly. 'I'm his brother and he's run away from home.'

'Yeah. And you got five other brothers down the tube there. What do you call yourselves? Bother brothers?'

Alfie smiled sweetly again. 'You're making a big mistake.'

'You're a big mistake,' said the young guard, and they walked past Alfie. Sam gave him another little wave and Alfie's smile turned into a sneer of hatred.

'I'll get you,' he said.

'So you keep saying,' said Sam cheekily.

He and the guard crossed the road and the nick was only a few yards away. He was safe, his plan had worked. Sam felt a surge of exultancy.

'Thanks,' he said. 'What's your name?'

'Delroy.'

'Thanks, Delroy.' He paused at the door of the nick. 'Will you come in? My dad's mate would want to thank you.'

'No way. I'm not going in there.' He turned away. 'Best of luck, kid.'

'Thanks again.'

90

Delroy darted away across the road and Sam went inside. He felt he should have been accompanied by a fanfare of trumpets.

Once inside the police station, Sam walked purposefully up to the desk sergeant and said:

'Can I speak to Detective Inspector Frost?'

'And what would you be wanting him for, young man?' The burly middle-aged policeman grinned at Sam in an off-putting way, but Sam had not come so far to be put off.

'I've got an important message for him.' Sam's voice had a ring of confidence in it and the desk sergeant paused. A glint of recognition lit his eye.

'Aren't you –'

'I'd like to speak to Detective Inspector Frost,' repeated Sam, firmly overriding him. He didn't want to talk about Dad. Not here and not to this stranger who patronised kids.

'OK. I'll see if he's in.'

He went away, leaving Sam to look round the nick. There wasn't much to see. A young policeman clacked away at a typewriter in a corner behind the desk and there was a smell of stale uniforms and chips. The walls were covered with posters and offered rewards for missing animals and demands for missing children and appeals for information about suspects. Various officers were coming and going, changing shifts probably and pouring in and out of the back door. They brought with them the smell of the streets and a feeling of uncertainty. Some of them looked at Sam as if they recognised him and indeed they probably did. But Dad had not invited many of his mates home – not with Mum the way she had been. They'd only met when Dad had taken him down the nick or on the football field. If only Mum could have been the way she was now – then. In Dad's time, thought Sam. If only she could have been his new mum, or second mum, as Sam was now beginning to think of her.

A few minutes later a big rangy man dressed in sports coat and dark trousers pushed his way through the surge of coppers. His shirt was white and he wore highly polished black shoes. He was a lot older than Dad and had a thatch of silvery hair that was beginning to recede. He was every inch a copper, thought Sam, despite the fact that he was wearing plain clothes. Somehow it was the style of these so-called plain clothes that marked him out. Only coppers wore shoes and shirts like that. Sam could spot them at once, and wondered if the villains could as well.

'Sam?'

'Yeah.'

'Recognise me?'

'Bill Frost?'

'That's your man. How are you?'

'OK.'

'What can I do for you?'

He was standing and looking down at Sam curiously, legs planted wide apart. A few inches away the desk sergeant was busying himself with a ledger, but Sam knew he was listening. Even the young copper had stopped his staccato typing.

'I've got something for you.'

'Yes?' He showed no signs of moving, and simply seemed to plant his big polished feet even wider apart. Sam looked around him furtively. Was the bent copper around? Listening to what they were saying?

'Can we go somewhere on our own?'

The young policeman started typing again at a furious pace and the desk sergeant seemed to sigh and rattle at his ledger in disappointment.

'Sure.' Sam felt a great sense of relief. 'Come on.'

With surprising agility the big man led him past the vast hulk of the desk sergeant, through the outer office and up a flight of stone stairs that rang to the sound of Detective Inspector Frost's flinty shoes. Sam hurried to keep up with him.

They eventually arrived in a very small, bleak office with a tired-looking rubber plant and a heavily-stained table.

'Shoot.' Frost smiled at him encouragingly from across the table and Sam blurted into speech. As he spoke he stared fixedly at a calendar for a tyre company that displayed a rather ancient-looking lady in a bathing costume. The caption read IN THE SWIM.

When Sam transferred his gaze back to Bill Frost, the big man was looking at him very intently indeed, and when he got to the bit about the envelope and then produced it, Frost almost grabbed at it, half tearing it in his desire to get at the contents. Then he slowly read the papers that Albino Man had so carefully gathered together. After what seemed a very long time, Bill Frost put the documents down and gazed steadily at Sam.

'Do you believe me?' Sam asked, almost defensively.

Frost nodded. 'Yes, son, I believe you. But if I did have any lingering doubts Albino Man would clear them away. Of that I can assure you.'

'He's a good grass.'

Frost grinned. 'Right copper's son you've turned out to be. Yeah – he's my best.'

Sam felt a rush of elation.

'You've been through a lot, son. Haven't you?'

Sam didn't reply and he suddenly felt his lip trembling as if he was going to cry. Somehow he forced back the tears.

'Your dad was one of the best.'

'This bent copper,' Sam's voice was still very unsteady, 'who is he anyway?'

Frost shook his head, and Sam saw that for the first time he looked almost afraid. There were little beads of sweat on his forehead. 'You know I can't tell you that, son.'

'But he's going to be nicked, isn't he? I mean, after all that's happened.'

'He'll be nicked all right.' He paused for a long time and then said quietly: 'I've had my doubts. But your dad was very, very certain. Now we know for sure.'

'Does that evidence properly shop him then?'

Frost nodded. 'I think you can say that, son. In fact you definitely can say that.'

'Now?'

'I'm going to proceed against him. But I need to talk to my colleagues first. And then to some people higher up.'

'You won't let him do a bunk. To Spain or somewhere?'

Bill Frost grinned and then the smile faded abruptly from his face. 'He won't be doing a bunk anywhere, son. Not anywhere.' He paused, frowning, and Sam suddenly remembered.

He sprang to his feet. 'What are we sitting here for? Albino Man's in dead stuck at the cinema.'

Bill Frost picked up the telephone. 'Don't you worry, son. Albino Man can look after himself. He's got a hidey hole.'

'S'pose they find it?'

But Frost was already barking instructions into the telephone.

'I've sent the area car round to check on him and make sure that your nasty little friend and his mates aren't nosing round the premises. And now I'm going to ring your mum.'

'Oh.' Sam was dismayed for he had been counting on going out to Wimbledon that afternoon. For now the urgent business was over, he wanted to do as he had planned. Go to Winston and his mother and there find something more of Dad.

'We'll get you down the railway station in a car and then get you picked up the other end. OK?'

'OK,' said Sam without enthusiasm. Then, partly out of curiosity and partly to try and play for time, he asked:

'Mr Frost?'

'Yes?'

'Who is Albino Man? What's his real name?'

''Fraid I can't tell you that, son.'

'Is that because he's a grass?'

'Something like that.'

'Oh.'

Frost's hand went to the phone and he asked Sam for his number. Sam fished it out of his back pocket and told him. As Frost busily dialled, a plan began to form in Sam's mind. It was risky but then he was used to taking risks by now.

'By the way . . .'

Sam was sipping a cup of tea that Bill Frost had brought in for him. It was hot and sweet and comforting but nowhere near as hot and sweet and comforting as Albino Man's had been. And come to think of it, he could do with one or six of his bacon sandwiches right now.

'Yes, Mr Frost?' said Sam dutifully.

'Why don't you call me Bill. Or Uncle Bill if you like.' He gazed at Sam kindly and Sam tried to smile back. But as he did so something very strange associated alarmingly in his mind. Uncle? Uncle Bill? Uncle George? The bent copper? Why – anyone could be that bent copper and suppose Albino Man had made some awful mistake and told Frost that – it was someone else when it might be Frost himself. Not Uncle George, but Uncle Bill? It was a terrifying and ridiculous thought. How could this big reassuring man be a villain? It was mad. But so had everything else been mad in the last few days. Suddenly Sam saw Uncle Bill reach in his pocket. He pulled out a small cigar and lit it as he waited for Sam's mum to answer the phone.

But once he was in the police car and speeding through the traffic, Sam completely dismissed the suspicion. He must be getting very tired to give poor Bill Frost all the attributes of the fantasy figure of his dreams. Now his risky plan took root and strength in his mind. It was a way – the only way – to get to Wimbledon. And getting to Wimbledon counted with him more than anything in the world right now. Dad was there, a new bit of Dad that he had never experienced before. He had to go and nothing was going to stop him, not even the Old Bill.

When they arrived at Charing Cross the two coppers bought him a hamburger, coke and some comics and put him on the train. He could see them discreetly checking out the train and the platform for any sign of Alfie and his gang, but they made one mistake. They didn't wait for Sam's train to pull out. They told him a car would meet him at Hastings and would take him home, and with that they left him to sit in the carriage until the train departed. And that was their big mistake.

Directly Sam was sure that his police escort had left, he did a very discreet and furtive bunk, edging out of the train, the platform and the station with many a scared look-out for the police. He was now more wary of them than Alfie or the bent copper or anyone else, but there was no sign of any police at all and at last Sam found himself half-running and half-walking down Villiers Street towards the Embankment Tube Station. Once there, he looked round again and nearly passed out. A policeman was walking towards the barrier. But then, when he thought that his heart had definitely stopped beating, the ghastly pounding and hollowness went away as he saw that the policeman was a stranger to him and was obviously from a completely different nick. With trembling hands, Sam fished out some money and went to the booking office. He asked for a ticket to Wimbledon. For some reason he did not think to ask for a return.

Part Six
Happy Families

'Hallo?'

The other end crackled and Sam recognised Tim's voice.

'It's Sam.'

Tim sounded gleeful. 'You aren't half in trouble. The police phoned Mum about you. He was a mate of Dad's and he said . . . '

'Did he say I'd solved it all?'

'Eh?'

Sam's voice was tinged with growing impatience. 'Didn't he say we were safe?'

'Eh?'

'It's all over. No one's going to hurt us ever again. I found the bent copper. At least, Albino Man did.'

'You barmy?'

'No.'

'What you on about, Sam? You been drinking? I don't understand a word you say. Mum's in a right lather. You bunked off and –'

'Listen –' Sam was desperate now. 'Get me Nan.'

'You should –'

'I said get me Nan.' Sam tried to make his voice sound as commanding as possible, but it didn't seem to work. Not with Tim.

'You ought to speak to Mum. I'll get her.'

'No.'

'Eh?'

'For Christ's sake get Nan. It's urgent.'

At last his urgency got through and Tim started to yell for Nan. Sam panicked. Suppose Mum came? What would he say? She'd never give him the address. There was a lot of shouting the other end and a voice came on. It sounded old and tired and Sam knew it was Nan.

'I'll just get Mum,' she said and disappeared. Sam could have screamed aloud and almost did. Just wait till he got home. Tim had a few things coming to him all right. And they wouldn't be nice. Not nice at all. Sam almost put the phone down when he heard his mum's voice, but he didn't.

'Sam?'

'Yeah.'

'Where are you?'

'In a call box.'

'You should be on the train. Bill Frost phoned and said that –'

'I know. I did a bunk.'

'You silly boy! Why?' Strangely her voice seemed quite calm

'I want to go to Wimbledon.'

She was quiet for a moment and when she spoke again he thought that he could hear a sob in her voice. But it was barely discernible and otherwise she seemed very controlled. 'What am I going to say to the police, Sam?'

'Tell them.'

'Isn't that just what we're trying to keep away from them? Wimbledon and all.'

Sam went rigid. Of course. Now why hadn't he thought of that?

'You're letting your dad down. You're being selfish, Sam.'

'It's all right, Mum. I've solved it. They got the bent copper. You should be pleased. No one's gonna hurt us any more.'

But like Tim she didn't understand, or she wasn't thinking. And selfish or not he was going to Wimbledon and to hell with the consequences.

'Listen, Mum, I'm going. Tell the coppers I jumped the train to see a mate and I've phoned you to say I'm safe. Then they'll never find out about Wimbledon.'

'They won't like it.'

'I don't care. And Mum –'

'Yes?'

'Can you give me the address? You must know it.'

There was a short silence, and when she spoke again, he was sure he could hear that slight sob in her voice. 'Sam –'

'Yeah?'

'Are you really sure you want to go?'

'I'm really sure, Mum.'

'Will you come straight back? On an early train tonight?'

'Yes, Mum.'

'Promise?'

'I promise, Mum.'

'It's 96 St James's Drive. Near the station, by a big old-fashioned pub.'

'Thanks.'

'Promise you'll get that early train?'

'I told you I would.'

'Sam –'

'Yeah?'

'Best of luck.'

Sam felt a very warm glow. 'Bless you, Mum.'

'I love you, Sam.'

'I love you, too, Mum.'

He put down the phone because he couldn't bear any more and the tears started out of his eyes as he walked away from the telephone box.

St James's Drive was a narrow street that ran between the station and a large old-fashioned public house. The houses were Victorian and each had a small front garden that was composed of dusty privet hedge, rockery and a large number of cracked paving stones. The front doors had coloured glass panels above them, and there was an atmosphere of cheerful respectability. As he walked up the road, Sam saw that many of the houses had lace blinds at the windows and one or two of them were tweaked discreetly aside as he passed by.

Number 96 was a little trimmer and a little tidier than any of the other houses and they were all smart. There were no lace blinds but coloured curtains at the window and window boxes at the front. The paving stones had been mended in the front garden and a BMX bike leant up against the front door which was ajar. Sam hesitated and then opened the smartly-painted garden gate and went up to the front door. He felt oddly calm and confident as he approached it. There was a plaque to the right of the door and it read SUNNYBANK. Somehow, despite the wintry day, the name was just right.

Sam knocked at the door with the highly polished brass knocker, but there was no reply and there seemed complete silence from within despite the fact that the door was slightly open. He knocked again and there was still nothing. Eventually and almost by some instinct he pushed open the door and looked into a neat and welcoming hallway. There was polished brass gleaming on the walls and a little table with a model of a gingerbread cottage on it. Sam felt so strange here; rather like he had felt on a school trip to the British Museum. They had been glad to look at the treasures of people's past. Now here he was looking at Dad's. It felt so right to be here and the cottage itself seemed to glow in the early afternoon sunshine. It was a hump-backed cottage with two bow windows and the clay modelling was so good that Sam could almost taste the gingerbread. Then he noticed that there was a miniature sign fixed to the gate of the cottage. It read SUNNYBANK.

There was still no sign of anyone, but the loud ticking of a clock drew him to an equally neat front room. The clock began to chime but it did not alarm Sam in the least. Once again it just seemed so right. Then bitterness overcame him – and he almost retched. It was as if Mum and Nan had stood for nothing – had created nothing for Dad. Not even a home. Here, everything was so neat, so polished, so welcoming and so special. Then he saw Dad's photo. Not one but four. They were ranged around on a number of little tables and each one was draped with a black band. Dad was in uniform in one of the photos, but in the other three he was relaxing with a comfortable-looking black woman. She was quite short and quite fat and she smiled in a way that Sam instantly liked and loved. Winston was in one of the two other photographs. They were on a beach somewhere that Sam did not recognise. Dad had picked Winston up and was running towards a sunlit sea. Sam felt a terrible unease. He liked Winston but he was afraid of how well he had known Dad. But he had to ask Winston – and go on asking him until these parts of Dad lived for him too.

They were certainly good photographs, despite their sad black bands. He looked round and out of the window.

He assumed that Auntie and Winston were just down the road getting some shopping, although it was funny that Winston had left his bike and that Auntie had left the front door open. Anyone could have got in. Like he had. Sam looked round the room again. The shelves were packed with books and more photographs and Sam saw Dad was in most of these as well. There was a big deep sofa and on the wall pictures of quiet coves and two of what he thought must be an island in the West Indies. It had palms and a deep blue sea and a little baby playing on the beach. Perhaps it was Winston. He hoped it was, for a reason he didn't really understand. There was a big television set and a video recorder and Sam thought how nice it would be to sit here on winter evenings and watch the TV in the warm glow of the false fire that cosily threw false flames across a false pile of logs. The flames would never burn this house down, he thought.

Sam yawned and sat down on the sofa. He would wait for them to come back from the shops. They would come soon. But would they welcome him? And should he feel he belonged? Sam slept uneasily, his eyes slipping drowsily away from the photographs of Dad into a dream where Dad walked into the room and ignored him completely. Then he saw Winston sitting on the rug. Dad ran his hands through Winston's hair. Let's go and play in the garden before tea, he said, and Winston nodded and got up. They went into the garden and Sam watched them through the window. It was quite big but didn't have any grass. It had sand and palm trees and a warm winking blue sea some distance away. They played with the football on the beach. And Sam went on watching. Then, Winston and Dad ran shouting after the football and into the shallows of the great warm blue sea. A starfish floated towards them and they waded further out, shouting and pushing each other in and out of the light blue waves. The sea grew deeper but they played on, ducking each other below the cooler water and seeing the shadows of fleecy clouds above them. Sam found himself rigid and stationary in the chair. Then he was on the floor of the ocean and he could see the legs of Dad and Winston waving above him. There were rocks and trailing seaweed and a few bloated-looking fish and the most enormous crab that Sam had ever seen. In the icy water he floated towards it, and then he saw that instead of having antennae it had a face. Despair filled him as he made out the foxy, pallid features of his old enemy Alfie.

Sam woke up and stared into Alfie's face. Alfie. Here. It wasn't possible. Couldn't be possible. But nevertheless here he was. He was grinning, yellowish teeth very much to the fore, and in one hand he gripped a piece of iron bar. He stank of sweat, but behind the grin Sam suddenly read the fear in his eyes. Still unbelieving, Sam staggered to his feet.

'Don't try anything, you little sod.' Alfie brought back his fist and punched Sam so hard in the face that a kind of grey film swam in front of his eyes and he tasted blood and teeth. As he fell back on to the sofa Alfie kneed him in the stomach and he gave a tiny little gasp as all the breath was knocked out of him.

At first Sam thought he was going to die. He just couldn't breathe and it seemed to last so long that he could feel himself blacking out. Then, very gradually, his breath came back in little spasms and he sobbed with the pain of it all. As normal vision returned he saw Alfie standing over him, perhaps waiting to have another go at him. Sam doubled his legs up on the sofa and took refuge in howling childish tears. He saw his dad in the photographs and prayed that his ghost would come back and do over Alfie. But there were no such things as ghosts. At least, not when you wanted them anyway.

'Shut up.'

But Sam continued to howl.

'You go on and I'll give you another one.'

Sam stopped.

'Now get on your feet. Fast.'

Sam did as he was told.

'Walk in front of me.'

Sam struggled to his feet; clasping his bleeding mouth and thumbing a loosened tooth, he stumbled along in front of Alfie, praying that he would not kick or hit him again. But he quickly forgot himself when they arrived in the kitchen, for bound and gagged on the kitchen floor were the black woman in the photograph and Winston. Winston had a long cut on his cheek. Also in the kitchen, sitting quietly and enjoying the joke, were Alfie's mates. Some of the furniture had been smashed and there were broken cups on the floor.

'Go and close the front door,' said Alfie to one of his mates as he pushed past Sam.

'What are you going to do to us?' asked Sam. He was still in pain but the shock had been too great for him to know real fear.

'We got instructions,' said Alfie.

'What are they?'

'We been told to keep you lot tied up for the night.'

'The night?' He looked down at Winston and saw that his eyes were angry and defiant. Then Sam looked across at Winston's mother and he read in them the same fear that he had seen in Alfie's. A kind of wild hope surged through him. Why should Alfie be afraid? Could he be taking on something that he couldn't handle? Could the 'instructions' be too much for him? That was a hope on which they all might build.

Sam was taken roughly by one of the gang – a smaller but tough-looking boy – and tied up. They were using twine which cut horribly into his wrists and ankles, but it was not nearly as painful as the gag which was thrust into his already ravaged mouth with so much force that the pain was horrendous. Tears ran down Sam's cheeks and Winston's mum looked at him in mute appeal. Then one of the gang switched on the television and they sat down to watch an afternoon Western with the sound turned discreetly down. While the film ran, the gang sporadically raided the larder and wolfed down their food like animals. Sam felt sick but he tried to identify their names as he lay there. It was what Dad would have wanted him to do. For identification, if he ever got out of this mess. He heard in his mind the words 'Here's another fine mess you've got me into' and the figure of Oliver Hardy darted across his imagination.

Then everything changed very quickly, so quickly that Sam was beginning to wonder if he was living in some kind of crazy speeded-up film.

The television did it. Suddenly an announcer interrupted the film and one of the gang turned up the sound. The announcer looked grim-faced and urgent as he read the news flash:

'We interrupt this film with news of a shooting in South London. Reports are still coming in, but the information we have to date is that a plain-clothes policeman has been killed in a South London cinema. The manager has been severely injured and is in a critical condition. There will be a fuller report in the six o'clock news.'

They snapped the sound down and Sam stared up at Alfie's face. He looked grey-green with fear and apprehension. In a little voice he squealed:

'I don't want to have none of that.'

The gang seemed visibly shocked and stared at each other as if waiting for someone to do something or plan something, or at least to say something, but no one moved. They just gawped at each other while Sam's brain began to race. They could only be the two he knew. His thoughts became confused and then stood out in a dreadful crystal clarity. Oh, God. It was awful. Really awful. Bill Frost: dead? Albino Man: almost dead? It was unbelievable. But so was everything else. Sam felt that if the world suddenly ended here and now he wouldn't be particularly surprised.

Bill Frost dead? How? Did Alfie do it? How long had he been in the house? And if not Alfie – who? Suddenly Sam knew. It was Uncle George – the bent copper. Who was not Bill Frost. Who was someone else. Someone who was terribly dangerous because he was exposed. An animal at bay. Not an animal like Alfie but a really deadly one. But surely Bill Frost had told someone. Or had he not told anyone? Perhaps he had just gone down to the cinema to see Albino Man and he had been waiting in the darkness of the cinema. A man who had the authority to send other policemen away until he had to himself the only two people who knew the secret. The only two? Sam felt the vomit rising in his throat. There were three people who knew the man's identity – or he suspected of knowing it. One was dead, the other dying and the third was his mum.

Grunting and looking desperately at Alfie, Sam tried to say something, and failed. And the more he failed the more he saw Mum lying dead in the road outside the house in Hastings. And he saw Tim dead and Nan and

107

Auntie Sue. All lying in the road. All dead. He would have no one. No one in the world.

Meanwhile another of the gang, Tel, at last burst into halting speech, and as he threw the rest of his food down the sink, he looked as frightened as Alfie. He turned accusingly on him.

'You never said we'd get mixed up in anything like this. We could get a bleeding lifer for this lot.'

'Shut up.'

'I'm off.'

'Wait.' Alfie tried to bar his way and the others moved towards the two of them as they stood irresolute in the kitchen doorway. Then Alfie, groping for command, said:

'Set 'em free.'

Roughly the gang rushed at them, and in a few minutes Sam was on his feet and painfully rubbing at his wrists. Winston and his mum staggered to their feet although they were much stiffer than Sam.

'All right, Alfie,' said Sam quietly. 'What now?'

Alfie gazed at him helplessly.

'Who put you up to all this?'

'I dunno.'

'If you tell me it'll go easier for you. I'll be a witness.'

'You little bastard.' Alfie advanced on him and then paused, clearly thinking better of it.

Sam stood his ground. He had to save them all. Save them from joining Dad.

'Who put you up to this?'

There was a dead stillness in the kitchen and the stranger who wasn't a stranger, his dad's woman, stared at Sam in a wondering kind of way. Sam repeated: 'Who was it, Alfie?'

'I never knew the bloke. He was a copper though. Bent copper. We was told what to do by Frostie.'

The revelation was incredible.

'Bill Frost?'

'Yeah, he was the middle man, like. He paid us.' Alfie reflected, his lips moving soundlessly in his agony. 'It was good money,' he said by way of explanation.

'What did he ask you to do?'

'Frighten you off. Thought it would work at first.'

Then Sam had his brainwave. 'You know what?'

'What?' It was weird. Alfie was almost dependent on him now. Sam felt a surge of power.

'There's been killings already. You'll get years.'

Alfie trembled visibly and the rest of the gang looked as if they were going to throw up.

'But I could get you off the hook.'

'You?'

'Me. If I said you were gonna help out, like.'

'Help out.' Alfie kept repeating his words in a glazed sort of way and the others followed his lead. They were all looking at Sam in a terrible concentrated appeal.

'At the last ditch. You know where this guy's going. He's going to my mum.' Sam let out a terrible bellow and he repeated his awful cry. 'Going to my mum, right? To fix her. And to shut her up. And kill her. So no one will know who he is. He thinks she knows who he is. All the evidence –' Sam gasped for breath ' – Frost gave it him. But he killed Frost. He didn't have no use for him no longer. What do you think he'll do to you? If the Old Bill doesn't get to you first?'

'What do you want?' asked Tel in a trembling voice. Suddenly the gang looked like a bunch of little kids.

'Got your bikes?'

They nodded.

'Put 'em round the corner,' muttered Tel.

'OK. We want to get down there fast.'

'Eh?'

'We want to get down to Hastings. To help Mum. And fast. I want to go on the back of your bike, Alfie. And if you take me, I'll tell the Old Bill to go easy on you and your mates.'

Alfie nodded eagerly. So did the others.

'Wait a minute,' said a strange voice and Sam turned to look at Winston's mum speaking for the first time. It was a good voice, firm and sure. 'Why can't we call the police?'

'Not now,' said Sam gently. 'We can't trust the police.'

Alfie nodded enthusiastically. 'We can't trust the police,' he repeated after Sam, again like a dependent little kid.

She nodded and looked at Winston. 'I'm coming too. You can't leave me out. We're all in this together.' She nodded at him as if he were a man. It was the gang who were the kids, dependent and shambling. Humble purveyors of transport.

'Right,' said Winston's mum. 'Let's go.' She turned to Alfie. 'And you'd better drive carefully, son.'

Driving carefully was not Alfie's style and Sam was terrified as he sat on the back of the bike and gripped Alfie's bony waist. He had seen other boys sitting on the pillion without a care in the world, their hands idly holding on to their saddle. But Sam, without a crash helmet and freezing cold in the streaming wind, clung on to Alfie for dear life, although he still knew that he was very firmly in charge and that Alfie was his servant. In front of them he could see Winston's mum clinging on to Tel, and somewhere behind him he was sure that Winston was holding on, just as terrified as he was. It was strange this sudden sharing of danger with two people that he had thought about so much but knew so little of. But now he was only thinking of Mum and Tim and Nan and Auntie Sue and what might be happening to them. His only comfort was Auntie Sue. She was a woman of the world and might have a trick or two up her sleeve against the unwelcome attentions of Uncle George. As for Mum well, she might be a new mum but she wasn't that new. Surely she wouldn't have the strength to face up to him. And as for Tim and Nan, well, it didn't bear thinking about.

Somehow they negotiated the London streets without incident. It was dark now and the rush hour had built up all down the Old Kent Road, but the bikers swerved their way between the cars and always with an inch or two to spare they managed to brush through. Brushing was the word and when Sam looked at the hard shiny bodies of the cars and trucks and buses so near to his legs he shuddered and shut his eyes. But all he could feel was the heat of the exhausts and the oily wind rushing past him.

Once they were on the motorway, despite heavy traffic, Sam felt that he could relax a bit more. Their progress was steadier and the sensation of erratic speed and imminent danger ceased. Sam had mainly worried about being stopped by a police car. This was for a variety of different reasons – all of them unpleasant. But now, under a brightening crescent moon and a network of glimmering lofty stars, they were speeding along the black ribbon of the motorway in a curiously weightless way. He could smell the rancid silage from a dry yard and then the faint scent of bracken from a woodland. Soon they were over the brow of a hill and Sam could see the countryside stretched around him and the glow on the horizon of the distant sea. At least he thought it was and the image comforted him. We're coming, Mum, he muttered under his breath. We're coming, Tim. Hold on. Hold on. Hold on. The roar of the bike seemed to pick up the message. Please God, we're not too late.

They were. Nan opened the door to a flushed and breathless Sam and just looked at him in horror. He asked her again and knew that he was too late. She seemed to pick up his fear. Raw and relentless on the porch.

'There was a call from the police station. They said they were to come down. But –' she stared at Sam's set face ' – I wondered –'

'Where's Auntie Sue?'

'She's been out all day.'

Nan stared helplessly down at him, knowing instinctively that there was danger but feeling too old and too helpless to pin it down or to take a decision.

'Where are you going?' she asked miserably, gazing at the dark hosts of bikes as they revved up in front of the house.

'Down the nick,' said Sam and turned away. She watched him run towards the bikers, her world torn and broken. Under her numbness the fear clawed at her like the minute claw of a crab. They would all die. She would lose them all. She would be all alone.

At the nick the news was bad. The desk sergeant at Hastings police station stared down at Sam in surprise. 'Your mum and brother never came here. We didn't call 'em in.'

Sam didn't waste words. He just rushed out to his army outside.

'They're not there. They never called 'em in.' He gasped out the words, and Winston's mum tried to put an arm round him but he backed away. She smelled of the night, dark oak apple and bitter orange and he could sense her flinching at his rejection. Then he felt a hand on his arm and he inched himself round to see Winston. His smile was tender and appealing and oddly reassuring.

'We'll find them, Sam. Honest we will.'

Sam turned back to the bikers. 'Alfie,' he commanded.

'Yeah?' His voice was humble and whiny and unassertive. His eyes in the darkness looked like the eyes of a rabbit – mild and blue and milky.

'We gotta comb the town. Now.'

'Sure.'

The machine roared and Sam prayed as he had never prayed before. Oh Mum. Oh Tim. If there is a God, let him hold you. Keep you safe. Mum.

For what seemed hours they circled the town, and as they did so a cold drizzling rain fell on them and the road and the pavements, reducing everything to a wet glare. Then it stopped, to be replaced by a clammy mist that rolled in off the sea. Soon they could see little but intermittent neon and glistening muffled light. Then as they sped round the old town and the tall net-drying huts, Sam saw something that he recognised. Someone. It was Tim. Running. Running as he had never run before.

'He's got Mum.'

'Who?'

'The man.'

'God!'

They had all stopped and Tim cuddled into Sam and wept and shook, quite oblivious of the others and unquestioning of their presence.

'Where is she?'

'On the rocks.'

'The rocks?'

'I got away. Ran for help. But no one listens.'

'How long you been running?'

'Minute or two.'

'Right. Over there.' He glanced around to find himself staring up into the face of Winston's mum. He hesitated. But he knew he had to ask her. She was the only grown-up around anyway. 'Can you stay with him?' he asked reluctantly. 'Can you look after Tim?'

She nodded and he quickly looked away.

Then Sam slapped Alfie's leather-jacketed back.

'Go to the rocks.'

Alfie did as he was bid and Winston's mum stood and stared after them as they all roared off. Momentary panic swept her. Then she began to run through the curling swathes of mist towards the old town, dragging Tim behind her.

'Where we going?' he yelled.

'To find a copper,' she said. They ran into the whiteness and disappeared as if swallowed up from the face of the earth.

The rocks looked like sleeping toads, insubstantial in the white fleeting mist. He could see no sign of water, but a gentle sighing made Sam aware of its presence. Now he wished they had brought Tim. What a dreadful mistake. Where was Mum? They stopped the bikes in the pebble-strewn car park and there was an awful silence. They began to run. Sam was racing beside Winston and the two were matching their strides pace by pace as they crunched painfully over the pebbles. Just behind them they could hear the gasping and panting of Alfie and Tel and the others.

Suddenly they were in another car park, and over by the pebbles there was a single car. It was near the sea line and for a moment Sam thought that it contained a snogging couple. There were two figures on the back seat, hard-etched in an embrace. Then one of the figures seemed to slump away and the other got out. He left the door open and tossed something in. And then something else. It was a few seconds before Sam realised that he was striking matches and he was so intent on his purpose that he was quite oblivious to them as they ran over the pebbles towards him.

Then the man stepped back as the car burst into flames.

'Mum!' Sam roared out the word, instinctively knowing what was happening. Once again he felt Winston beside him, and the man turned and gaped at them as they sprinted towards the roaring flames of the car.

'Get him,' yelled Winston as Sam wrenched open the door of the car, and he heard Alfie's answering whine. The man began to run and then neither Winston nor Sam could think of anything else but the roaring of the flames and the figure that was slumped across the back seat of the car. The heat was so intense that Sam could smell his own hands and hair singeing as they tried to drag the lumpen, burning figure out of the car.

Eventually they succeeded in getting her out, and she lay some feet away from the car, her face blackened and her clothes still burning.

'What can we do?' howled Sam. 'My mum's burning.'

'You do this,' muttered Winston and flung himself on top of her. Backwards and forwards Winston rolled over her, smothering the flames, and Sam saw again his home burning and now his mum burning and now Winston burning. Their figures swelled in size and then diminished. He passed out.

Sam woke up to the sound of an ambulance siren and the flashing of police car lights. They seemed very near him. He rolled over painfully and saw Mum lying on a stretcher. Sam pulled away from a policewoman's grip and crawled over the stinging pebbles towards her. Her face was black – black like Winston, who was nowhere to be seen. Then Sam saw Winston's mum and Tim bending over her and they were crying and laughing at the same time. Slowly Mum parted her cracked and blackened lips and smiled at him.

'I'll be all right, Sam.'

'She will,' said Winston's mum and her voice was strangely, almost irritatingly reassuring.

Painfully Sam got to his feet. His jeans were stinging now and he knew that they were burnt.

'Stay with me, son.' The policewoman grabbed at him again but he slipped away from her and began to run across the pebbles. The mist had cleared now and he could see clearly in the moonlight. Once again he was reminded of his own house burning as he heard the radios murmuring and the pips bleating and the fire engine on the foreshore and the firemens' hoses playing on the smouldering wreck of the car.

Then he saw another group of policemen with the bikers, and for a moment he thought that Alfie and Co were being arrested. His attention was caught by a tall man handcuffed to two policemen, being led towards one of the flashing police cars. Sam ran towards him and the policemen stopped momentarily. As Sam came up, the moonlight picked out the features of a man with a gentle face and a small wispy moustache. Despite the handcuffs he still looked authoritative. He was wearing a tweed suit and strong brown brogues and a raincoat and looked as if he ought to be smoking a pipe if his hands had not been so

116

firmly locked together. As this thought flashed into his mind Sam caught a strong whiff of some rich dark tobacco. Funny, thought Sam, he ought to smell of cigar smoke.

Sam walked right up to the man and stared into his face and still the police paused. Their eyes met and Sam saw that they too were gentle and kindly. Strange what gentle kindly men will do if they're desperate, he thought.

'So you're Uncle George,' said Sam.

Part Seven
An Old Friend

Sam, Mum and Winston went to the local hospital in Hastings to have their burns dressed, and then they were taken to another hospital in London which was near the temporary accommodation on the estate that the council had given Mum. It also had a good burns unit. But it was only after Sam had been there for a couple of days that he remembered. This was the hospital that Wes was in. The thought took some getting used to. But the pain soon overcame the thought of Wes's presence, for Sam's hands needed a good deal of treatment. Mum had severe burns and would need to stay in hospital for some weeks, though she was not in any kind of danger. As for Winston, he had nasty burns too and would need to stay in at least as long as Mum. He was a hero, Sam was told. And Sam agreed.

Winston's mum came to the hospital every day and Sam was polite to her. She tried to be warm, but he remained distant. It would be good to see Winston when he got out, but he wasn't so sure about his mum. He only had time now for his own. Sam had responsibility now and they were going to have a new life without Dad. A new life that was going to be very different – and very hard. It was a fresh start with Mum who deserved and would receive his love and reassurance. And he would help her look after Tim and Nan. They all needed him. The past, he knew, was like a big clumsy animal, waiting to knock them down directly they could stand up. And they weren't strong enough for that yet.

Sam began to dream about Dad again and they were good dreams, full of memories that were vivid and real. Once another face crept into his dream – Albino Man – and when he woke up, Sam wondered if he was alive or dead. He wanted very much for him to be alive.

Sam went to see Wes. They were pleased to see each other. Wes looked much better, sitting out in his wheelchair, and he was obviously not in such pain. Even the nurse seemed pleased to see Sam and she winked at him as she passed.

'So you got yourself out of that mess, then?' said Wes curiously.

Sam grinned and told him the whole story in vast detail.

'So your dad's in the clear,' he said when he'd finished.

Wes nodded but didn't say anything.

'What about Albino Man?' asked Sam curiously, feeling suddenly tense. He couldn't bear him to be dead. But could he expect him to be alive?

'Him.' Wes appeared to have difficulty in saying anything at all. Then he muttered, 'He's off the danger list, they say. Going to be all right.'

Sam whooped with joy and then stared down at Wes's unhappy features.

'Everyone's OK except me,' he whispered, staring up at Sam as if he were trapped.

Sam went over to the wheelchair and gave Wes a friendly punch. A tear ran down Wes's cheek but they both pretended it wasn't there.